Pizzicato

Pizzicato
The Abduction of the Magic Violin

Rusalka Reh

TRANSLATED BY David Henry Wilson

amazon crossing

Pizzicato - The Abduction of the Magic Violin by Rusalka Reh was first
published in 2009 by Verlag Friedrich Oetinger as *Pizzicato oder Die
Entführung der Wundergeige*.
Cover art by Eva Schöffmann-Davidov.
Translated from German by David Henry Wilson.
First published in the U.S. in 2011 by AmazonCrossing.

Published by AmazonCrossing
P.O. Box 400818
Las Vegas, NV 89140

ISBN-13: 9781611090048
ISBN-10: 1611090040

Every blade of grass has its angel, who bends over it and whispers to it: "Grow, grow."

The Talmud

My warmest thanks to Claus Derenbach,
master violin-maker, for allowing me to watch and learn
in his magnificent workshop.

CHAPTER ONE
Auto Frederick Is Cool

"Darius Dorian!" Mrs. Helmet waves an envelope around in the air, and it looks like a fluttering dove. She quickly grabs her coat and glances at her wristwatch. "Hurry up, will you, just for a change, or my train'll leave without me in fifteen minutes' time! You're last!"

"*It's* last!" hisses a freckled boy in the front row. His name is Max, and he's class president and self-proclaimed Darius-hater. He grins.

A boy in the back row stands up and walks toward the teacher's desk. He walks quite slowly, as if he's forgotten exactly why he stood up and started moving. He's almost gotten as far as the teacher when he trips over something. He stumbles, grabs hold of the edge of the desk, and ends up standing in front of the teacher like a car after a particularly difficult parking maneuver.

"Dear oh dear!" cries Mrs. Helmet, shaking her head. "You and an Australian wombat would really make a fine couple! You know what usually happens to those poor creatures? They get *run over* because they're so slow. You do everything slower than any other child I know, including falling over!"

Everybody giggles, Max loudest of all, since it was actually he who had furtively stuck out his leg.

"Here," says Mrs. Helmet and hands the envelope to Darius. "This contains the address of *your* project site." She hurriedly slips on her coat. "As you all know, this is the first time our school's tackled a project like this, and it depends entirely on your good behavior whether subsequent classes will be given the same treat. So behave yourselves! I think you've all got everything you need. For those whose project sites are a long way from home, there are facilities on the spot for you to stay overnight. And keep in mind, you should take notes for your essay. The title is 'The Work People Do.' And it should be at least eight pages long. Otherwise it just won't be worth all the expense."

Mrs. Helmet throws her bag over her shoulder. "So we'll meet again at the beginning of May—that's three weeks from now. Bye!"

"Byeee!" trills the chorus.

When the bell rings, their teacher has already disappeared.

Of course, Darius had guessed that on the way home Max would start getting at him. The two of them live in the same place, The Stork's Nest Children's Home. Unfortunately, they not only live in the same home, which is bad enough in itself, but they even live in the same house, although there are actually *nine* houses on the campus. And to top it all…they even share a room. The boy Darius hates more than anyone else in the world sleeps in the bunk bed above his and every night and every morning flaps his bare feet extra loud up and down the rungs of the ladder six inches away from Darius's face.

"Well? Where you goin', slugboy?" Max asks him now. The April sun is shining onto his freckled face. He makes a grab for the envelope, which is poking out of Darius's jacket pocket.

Darius quickly puts his hand on it. A cold gust of wind suddenly blows through his hair, and the trees at the side of the street throw harsh shadows onto the walls of the houses.

"Don't know yet," he says. It's true. He still hasn't opened the envelope.

Max says cockily, "I'm with Auto Frederick! Cool, huh?" He walks like Arnold Schwarzenegger, top-heavy. "Nothin' but Porsches an' stuff. Only the best cars fer Max."

Darius nods and kicks a stone. "Good for you."

"Oh, come on!" yells Max, standing still. "Gooood?" He towers up in front of Darius, legs astride and forefinger pointing. "Auto Frederick is *cool*, slugboy. Can't you get that into yer sluggy brain?"

A veil of clouds now draws itself across the blue sky, and the sun disappears behind it.

"Yeah," whispers Darius.

"*What* is Auto Frederick, Mr. Moron?" asks Max, digging his finger deep into Darius's ribs. It really hurts.

"Auto Frederick is cool," whispers Darius, and suddenly his hands feel cold and damp.

♪ ♪ ♪ ♪ ♪ ♪

"Hi, you two! So tell me, did you manage to avoid killing each other on the way home?"

A man with a long ponytail and a hooded sweatshirt is sitting in the hall of House Four, putting a pair of pink gym shoes on a little girl.

Without answering, Max goes past him and thumps his way upstairs. At the top he yells, "Auto Frederick, everybody! The coolest of the cool!"

Darius heaves his schoolbag off his shoulders. Ben is his favorite carer, and Darius is pleased that he's still on duty.

"And where are they sending *you*, Darry?" asks Ben, tying a double knot in the little blonde girl's shoelace. "Done," he says.

Darius feels for the envelope in his jacket pocket. "Don't know," he says again.

"Tighten my belt!" whines the little girl. She is seven years old, but looks no more than four: very small and thin. Since her mother put her in the home, she hasn't grown a single centimeter. She wants to stay this small so that her mother will still know her when eventually she comes to fetch her. In fact, her mother hasn't visited her even once in three years.

"You can hardly breathe even now, Queenie!" says Ben.

Queenie stamps her foot and tugs at her pink belt. She tightens it herself, by no less than two notches. Then she looks defiantly at Ben and disappears outside.

Darius is always surprised when Ben stands up, unfolding himself like an accordion. He's huge! Darius would also like to be that big. Then everyone would be sure to leave him in peace, including even Max.

"Food in half an hour," says the giant as he makes his way toward the kitchen. "Then will you tell us where they're sending you for this…this project?"

"Mhm," murmurs Darius and goes upstairs, where he can hear Max's voice yelling from their room.

"Wee-ooh! Moron alarm!"

When Darius enters the room, Max is crouching on the floor poking his friend Daniel in the side. "Just look at that stupid old granddaddy jacket he always wears!"

Daniel gurgles, as if on command. "Is baby going to have his little afternoon nap now?" he asks.

Oh God! Two against one. Cowards. Darius drops his schoolbag beside the desk and picks up his radio. If only they'd leave him alone! Or if he could just have his own room. If, if, if. In silence he takes off the large jacket that he'd fished out of the donations bag, and which he rather likes, takes off his sneakers as well, and flops down on his bed. Recently he's been doing that every day. Or let's say he's been doing it since last December. That was when he'd found the radio in the Christmas gift box, among the battered stuffed animals, jeans, remnants, T-shirts, and at least a hundred tattered comics. Mrs. Lewis, the secretary, had simply said he could have the radio. He had no idea why she'd been so nice to him that day. Anyway, now it's his, and only his, and nobody else's.

Okay, so it's pink, which admittedly doesn't look all that impressive, but it works. It works perfectly.

Darius pulls the comforter over himself and his radio.

"Come on, let's go," Max says to Daniel. "What a pain, that guy!"

The door slams shut.

Darius turns on the radio. At first there are some scratchy noises until he finds his favorite program, but then the music comes loud and clear through the speaker.

He pricks up his ears. Violin music!

And at that moment something rises up inside him, from his feet right up to his hair. He doesn't know exactly what it is, but whatever it is, it's something great.

Darius folds his hands behind his head and closes his eyes. But he's wide awake.

"That," purrs a woman's voice after a while, "was chamber music for violin, viola, and cello, the String Quartet in D Minor, Köchel Number 421 by Wolfgang Amadeus Mozart. It was played by the Tetzlaff Quartet and recorded at a performance—"

"Food!"

Darius starts. The deep voice of the giant Ben reaches into the furthest nook and cranny of House Four. From all directions you can now hear children's footsteps and voices.

Darius quickly switches off his radio, burrows his way out of his comforter tent, and takes the white envelope from his jacket pocket. He tears it open.

Design and decoration—Alice Ponticello, he reads.

That's his three-week project.

In a jeweler's shop.

Oh no! Unbelievably awful! And an absolute gift for his arch enemy, Max!

♪ ♪ ♪ ♪ ♪ ♪

"Good Lord, Jessica!" grumbles Ben. "You really don't have to go and shovel three pounds of it onto your plate! There's plenty for everyone!"

There are ten children sitting at the long, brightly colored wooden table in the dining room. The pot of hot dogs is steaming, and there's also the smell of potato salad with pieces of apple in it.

"Enjoy your meal," says Ben.

"Enjoy your meal," they all cry.

Then there's nothing but chewing, champing and chomping, and the clatter of knives and forks. Darius has his mouth full of hot dog with a forkful of potato-and-apple salad, which is his absolutely favorite meal, when the brief interlude of peace suddenly comes to an end.

"O' course I'll be drivin' a 911 Porsche at Auto Frederick." Max looks around, as if he's King of God-Knows-Where. Since nobody says anything, he clears his throat extra loud.

"So cool, man," he says as he takes another hot dog out of the pot and puts it next to the remaining half of his first one.

After a short pause of munching and crunching, Queenie says, "But you're only thirteen!" She's sitting next to Darius. "You're not even allowed to drive a car."

"Aaaargh!" shrieks Max and drops his knife and fork on the table with a clatter. "Nobody'll caaaare how old I am when I'm part of Auto Frederick, you stupid midget!"

"Max!" thunders the voice of the giant across the table.

Darius shoves some more potato salad into his mouth and chews it in silence. So long as nobody asks him where he's—

"So where are they sending *you*, Darry?" the giant promptly asks.

Max stops chewing and looks at Darius like a hyena waiting to pounce.

"Yes, that's right, where are *you* going?" Queenie asks as well.

There's no point. Some time or the other he'll have to tell them anyway, so why not now?

"Design and decoration, Alice Ponticello," he answers, and it sounds as if he's reciting some miserable advertising slogan.

For a moment there's silence.

"Awesome!" Max slaps his thigh and starts to laugh like crazy. He laughs and laughs until there are tears in his eyes. "Desaign and decorashun," he says with pursed lips. "Earrings an' gold chains, hoity-toity! Perfect fer our slugboy!"

He looks around, expecting a round of applause. A few children giggle quietly. Darius feels himself going beet red.

"Max, that's enough!" thunders Ben. "That's it for today. Go back to your room, please. I've had just about enough of you!"

Max stands up. But when Ben is busy eating again, he sticks his middle finger up at Darius and grins even more maliciously than before.

CHAPTER TWO

Three Tiny Weeks

♪♫

A t that very moment, in St. Matthew's Square at the other end of the town, an impressive-looking gentleman comes out of his house and slams the door behind him, which makes a sound like a clap of thunder. The house to which the high and heavy door gives access is more than a hundred years old, and the outside is covered with scrolls and patterns. To the left and right of the door hang two stone heads with mouths wide open. They look as if they're screaming. Beneath the stone face on the right is a brass plate bearing the inscription:

> ARCHIBALD ARCHINOLA
> MASTER VIOLIN-MAKER

With his coat billowing, the impressive-looking man hurries across St. Matthew's Square. He has a mane of curly hair on his head, over his eyes, and around his mouth. Black and silver-gray. One might not even see that there's a face behind that great bush were it not for his sparkling blue eyes.

He quickly crosses Buckle Street, skips onto the sidewalk, and hurries on. The wind blows his coat open, and for a moment he looks like a magician.

"Ah, Mr. Archinola, lucky I've bumped into you. May I come and practice with you again this afternoon?" cries a girl with a schoolbag, and then she looks bewildered as he simply rushes past her. Her straight black hair blows behind her because the man creates such a draft as he goes by. The girl has a brown patch on her neck and on her left hand, with which she now waves to the man behind his back. Her forefinger sticks up like a little wooden twig.

"Sorry, Mey-Mey, but I'm in a terrible hurry!" he calls to her over his shoulder. "Alice has a problem!"

He finally stops in front of a shop window and wipes his sweating brow with a linen handkerchief. Above the door of the shop it says:

DESIGN AND DECORATION
ALICE PONTICELLO

Huffing and puffing, he goes in.

He immediately sees his friend Alice, who is pacing up and down behind a glass counter, with the telephone to her ear and talking agitatedly. Her long dark hair with silver strands cascades down her sides as far as her waist, like a waterfall.

"No," she says, "no, and I can't think of anywhere else at the moment." She waves to Mr. Archinola, then turns her back to him and leans on the counter. "Look, surely you can find somewhere else for the boy instead of with me." She falls silent. "I see. He's one of those problem kids. From the children's home. Aha. I didn't realize that."

Mr. Archinola, still panting a little from his long-distance sprint, wanders along the glass display cases, wondering what's the matter with his friend. Normally she's quite unflappable. He knows, because he comes here every day, to look at her latest bits of jewelry. And also, secretly, to look at *her*. The fact is, Mr. Archinola is in love with Alice. He's been in love with her for seven years. Only he hasn't dared tell her.

While he patiently waits for her, his gaze falls on the corner with the plush red sofa. He catches his breath. How strange! There's a violin leaning against the wall. From a distance it looks like a really old one, thinks Mr. Archinola. *What's it doing here in Alice's jewelry shop?* Once again he stares at the violin, as if expecting it to politely introduce itself. It looks a funny color, bluish. Or maybe it isn't actually the violin at all, but a blue light falling on it from some lamp or the other. He's just about to go and take a closer look when Alice hangs up.

"I've made a right mess of everything," she says.

Mr. Archinola immediately forgets the violin, because he can hear from Alice's voice that she's on the verge of tears.

"What's the matter?" he asks. "I've been sprinting across half the town like a bat out of hell!"

Alice shuffles across to the corner with the sofa, where there's a wooden table with jewelry catalogs, a jar full of candy, and a nodding Chinese plastic cat, and she sinks down into the red plush. Mr. Archinola sits next to her.

"Mama's ill again," she begins. "You know, it's her heart."

Mr. Archinola nods. Last year Alice flew *three* times to Italy to see her sick mother, and *three* times he'd missed her terribly. Although, of course, she hadn't the slightest idea about that side of things.

Alice sounds even more tearful as she continues. "But there's a boy who's supposed to spend his job shadowing with me. I was actually looking forward to having him here." She sobs. "He would have come to me on Monday, but now I've got to turn him away, and the principal is furious because she doesn't know where she can get a place for him on such short notice, and…" She finally bursts into tears.

"There, there," mumbles Mr. Archinola, patting her on the shoulder. Then he gives her his handkerchief, because he's a real gentleman. He's simply forgotten the fact that he's just been wiping his sweaty brow with it. Alice blows her nose into it, trumpeting like a sad elephant.

"Archie?" she asks diffidently. "It's just a matter of… three tiny little weeks. They'll pass with a whoosh… Couldn't *you* take the boy on?"

Mr. Archinola leaps up as if he's sat on a thumbtack and only just noticed it. Indignantly he cries, "I have *ab-so-lutely* no time for silly games like that—you know I haven't!" He starts pacing up and down and stroking his beard. "Three tiny little weeks, with a whoosh! Really, Alice!" he mumbles, shaking his head.

"Oh, but the poor boy!" says Alice softly. "How's he going to face his classmates now?"

Mr. Archinola suddenly stops pacing. "What on earth have an unknown boy and his unknown classmates got to do with me?" he snaps. "I'm making a viola da gamba, for heaven's sake! Lord have mercy on us, it's going to take *months*, and it needs every second of my attention! And a kid like that...a problem child...he couldn't care less about my work!" He looks at Alice and snorts. "He'll...He'll be drinking Coke and spending all day long listening to his tralala-rumpety-boom-boom music. I can do without all that, thank you, Alice."

Alice looks at Mr. Archinola. She says nothing for a while.

Mr. Archinola goes on stroking his beard—which he always does when he needs to calm down, or when he has to think, or when he has to do both.

"Three tiny little weeks and...um...with a whoosh, you say?" he finally asks, breaking the silence.

"Oh, Archie!" Alice jumps up and flings her arms around her friend's neck. Without another word, she grabs hold of the telephone and presses redial. "Yes, it's Ponticello again, Alice Ponticello. What would you say to a violin-maker's for your boy's project?" She listens, then nods. "Yes, of course. And the boy will even have a bigger guest room than he'd have with me."

Guest room! Mr. Archinola had just finished calmly breathing in, and now, out of shock and horror, he forgets to breathe out again. The kid's supposed to *live* with him?

"Oh, I'm so relieved! Good-bye," says Alice and puts the phone down. "How can I ever thank you enough, Archie?" She smiles, and she's as radiant as one of the finest rubies in her shop window.

Mr. Archinola stares at her in complete silence. At the moment he's only thinking of one thing: whether, out of sheer love, he hasn't just made the biggest mistake of his life. Then his gaze falls once more on the corner with the sofa.

"By the way, what's this violin doing here?" he asks, picking it up.

"Oh yes, that," says Alice, "I'd almost forgotten it in all the excitement. A customer exchanged it yesterday for a silver chain. I didn't know him. He said he didn't have any cash."

Alice comes to stand next to Mr. Archinola, who gives the violin a professional once-over. "The chain was a discontinued line from the season before last," she explains, "not an expensive one, you know, and I thought maybe you might get some pleasure out of the violin. Do you like it?"

Mr. Archinola blinks and peeps through one of the f-holes. Then he turns the violin to and fro and holds it at arm's length.

"There's something special about it, yes," he murmurs. "Definitely something unusual." He turns to look at Alice. "It's a nice piece, and I'll put it in my collection for now. Then when I've got time, I'll restore it. It's certainly not valuable, but it's very beautiful. Thank you, Alice." He kisses her on the cheek and then immediately feels embarrassed.

"Have you bought a new lamp, by the way?" he asks, because he's just remembered the bluish light from a moment ago.

"No. Should I?" asks Alice, a little anxiously. "Do you think it's too dark in my shop?"

Mr. Archinola looks at the violin and then at the corner where it had been standing. If he had the slightest idea of what would soon be happening, he would certainly start mopping his sweaty brow again.

CHAPTER THREE
Just You Wait, Slugboy

Darius is hoping to avoid Max until the evening. Max really gets on his nerves. He'd like to go out on his bike now and do a bit of skidding and braking. But just as Darius is about to leave the house, the phone rings in the hall. Although he hardly ever gets any phone calls, he stands rooted to the spot, as if knowing that this call is for him. And when Ben picks up the receiver, Darius listens with ears pricked.

No doubt about it, the call *is* for him. It's for him and him alone and nobody else.

After a minute, Ben hangs up. "Ah, good, there you are!" he says.

Darius is really on tenterhooks now. In silence he looks at the giant. There's something important going on—he can sense it. And it's so important that he begins to feel dizzy.

"Don't look at me like that," says Ben, ruffling his hair. "It was only your school. This Lisa…Pontissimo, or whatever her name is, has suddenly had to go abroad somewhere."

Queenie comes running through the front door, and when she sees there's something exciting going on in the hall, she stops. "What's up?" she asks, wiping her nose.

"What's going on *here*?" asks Daniel, who also comes crashing through the door. "Plotting something, eh?"

"Nothing like that," says Ben. "The jewelry shop has fallen through, so Darius will be doing his project with a violin-maker. That's all. So now you can buzz off."

For a moment everything is swirling around in Darius's head. A violin-maker. But he can't tell one key from another.

"What's a violin-maker?" Queenie wants to know.

She always asks lots of questions because she thinks she's still only four, and kids ask lots of questions when they're four.

"Well, it's someone who makes string instruments that people can play music on," explains the giant.

"What are string instruments?" asks Queenie in a high-pitched squeak. When you're four years old, you must always ask another question after the first one, and preferably in a high-pitched squeak.

"Well, violins, for example," answers Ben.

"Cool!" says Queenie and looks at Darius with great respect. "Will you make a violin for me too, Darry?"

Now Darius realizes that there are quite a few children standing around in the hall. Suddenly the whole population of House Four has assembled. Or maybe not—there's one missing.

"Can he also make electric guitars?"

"Can I go to the violin-maker's too? Please!"

"Can we come and visit you there?"

Darius really hasn't a clue what's happening to him. A moment ago he'd been the miserable jewelry-shop slugboy, and now this. Suddenly he picks Queenie up and whirls her around in a circle. She squeals with pleasure and puts her head on his shoulder.

"Will you come back soon?" she asks, winding her thin arms around his neck.

"I haven't even gone yet!" whispers Darius. He can't help laughing. It all feels almost as nice as when he snuggles under the comforter with the pink radio.

"Where's my duffel bag?" Darius asks Ben and gently lowers Queenie to the floor.

"Back there in the garden shed," says Ben, smiling. "I expect it's all covered in dust. You can go and get it on Monday morning."

No one has noticed someone sitting in a dark corner by the staircase, listening to everything with a grim expression on his face.

"Just you wait, slugboy," he murmurs.

CHAPTER FOUR
Lilac and Woodlice

🎶

On Monday, the church bells in the distance are striking two o'clock when, from inside the garden shed at
the end of the Stork's Nest campus—where there are piles
of striped sunshades, deflated soccer balls, and several
suitcases—someone rattles the door.

"Open the door!" he shouts. "Open the door!"

In front of the door sits Max. He plucks a daffodil out
of the grass and sticks the stem between his lips. Then he
looks smugly around him. The sun shines into his eyes.

"Let me out! They're expecting me! I've got to be at
the violin-maker's at three. Please! I won't tell anyone you
locked me in!"

Max grins. The daffodil hangs out of the corner of his
mouth like a cigarette.

Cool, the way he's yelling, he thinks to himself. *Of course
they're waiting for him. You bet they're waiting!*

He stands up and spits out the flower. "Cheers, slugboy,"
he says quietly and disappears behind the lilac.

"Where the hell is Darius?" Ben is standing on the
veranda, looking agitatedly at his watch. "It's half past two
now, and we've got to go all the way across town. It'll take

at least an hour. Darry!" he shouts, cupping his hands in front of his mouth. "Daaaaarryyyyy!"

But Darius doesn't respond. Not now, not one hour later, and not even two hours later.

In the end, Ben picks up the phone and dials the number of Master Violin-Maker Archinola's workshop.

♪ ♪♪ ♪ ♪♪♪

"Yes, all right, I'm not deaf! I understand! Good-bye!"

Mr. Archinola slams the receiver onto the hook of his ancient telephone and lets out a loud snort as if trying to catapult two large boogers out of his nostrils. He takes off his stylish leather shoes, which he put on this morning especially in honor of the expected visitors, and slides his feet into his slippers. With vigorous movements he ties on his apron.

"Waste of time!" he mumbles, and stomps to his workbench. "What a nerve!"

He strokes his beard. Then he picks up his favorite saw.

"I knew this would happen! The kid's caused havoc even though he isn't here!" He begins to saw. "*Can't find him.* Don't make me laugh. And I stop work just for that, and go to all the trouble of tidying up my beautiful living room as a guest room for him!"

Furiously he saws on.

"And I even turned little Mey-Mey away because of him! And the poor girl has nowhere else to practice her violin!"

He doesn't take his eyes off the wood. He doesn't see that, in the display cabinet, where today he hung Alice's present, there is suddenly a soft blue light.

A long, thin, almost white piece of wood falls from the workbench onto the parquet floor. Mr. Archinola picks it up and examines it critically against the viola da gamba that he's making.

"That'll do nicely," he says, still looking grim-faced.

But this whole mess with the boy will not do nicely. *Well, he can forget about doing his project with me!* Mr. Archinola thinks to himself and switches on his bending iron to let it warm up. Then, frowning with concentration, he holds the thin slat of wood against it and with both hands slowly pulls the wood toward him, then repeats the action several times. He spends almost an hour doing this.

In the cabinet the blue light is getting stronger. Now it's shining through the glass doors down onto the floor, as if it were trying to make its way across to the man who is so busy at his workbench.

Apart from the church bells outside, there is not a sound in the workshop. The master violin-maker is still pretty angry as he broods over the letdown. And even now he hasn't noticed the blue light. The sun comes flooding through the tall south window, shedding a golden glow over the wooden objects—practically everything around Mr. Archinola is made of wood.

Finally, he picks up the slat, which now looks like a large *C*, and with bated breath he places it in the body of his model. Then he feels the weight of the head.

"Hm," he murmurs, and clicks his tongue. "The gamba mustn't be absolutely perfect, or it won't sound right, but it has to be almost perfect."

He goes to an ancient chest of drawers, takes out three screw clamps, and fastens the wood to the model. Then suddenly his face lights up with a smile.

"Almost perfect!"

With rapt attention, he gazes at his work. *Just wait till the viola da gamba is finished and shines forth in all its glory!* he thinks, and he can hardly wait for the great day.

"Just for you, my darling, I'll organize a *soirée musicale!*" he says aloud to the nascent viola, bowing as if to a princess and gently kissing the wood.

Mr. Archinola's musical evenings are famous throughout the town. As indeed are his wonderful musical instruments.

He has almost forgotten the missing visitor. And deep down he doesn't want him there anyway.

Why on earth did I let myself be talked into it? he asks himself, but of course he knows exactly why. "A donkey in love, that's me!" he grumbles at himself. "If the kid does come now, I'll tell him to go away."

For the first time in hours, Mr. Archinola straightens up, stretches, and looks around. The blue light in the cabinet has gone out.

♪ ♪ ♪ ♪ ♪ ♪

This evening, Queenie is riding around the Stork's Nest campus, balancing on her unicycle.

Suddenly she turns her head. Wasn't that someone shouting, back there, near the lilac trees? She strains to listen and tries to bring herself to a stop, which isn't easy. But now she can't hear anything, apart from the distant rumble of traffic down Park Avenue and the cawing of the pair of crows that live on the campus. But just as she starts to pedal again, she hears it once more.

There *is* someone shouting—she can hear it quite clearly now. He's shouting, "Help!"

Queenie pedals furiously, past House Eight and the trash cans behind the fence. When she reaches the garden shed, she jumps down. The unicycle falls silently onto the grass. She's pretty breathless now. She turns around. No one in sight. Silence. There are daffodils growing here, and it's like some beautiful magic garden. It all looks so peaceful.

"Hello! Is anybody there?" cries a voice from the garden shed.

It gives Queenie a shock. She wonders if the best thing wouldn't be to cycle off again at top speed. *Who knows what might be sitting in there?* she thinks. Maybe a criminal. Or a sorcerer, or a robot.

"Help! Open the door!"

Then Queenie recognizes the voice. "Darry?" she asks. "Is that you?"

"Fetch someone here, quick!" yells Darius. "I should have been at the violin-maker's ages ago!"

Instead of getting onto her unicycle, Queenie looks around with a frown. Finally, she picks up an ivy-covered flowerpot from the ground next to the door. A few terrified woodlice come scurrying out in all directions and crawl into the next best cracks. A key glints from underneath. Queenie smiles. A good thing she noticed that when she was watching Ben tidying the place up last autumn. Still smiling, she unlocks the door.

Blinking in the sunlight, Darius comes stumbling toward her. "How the heck did you manage to do *that*?" he asks.

Queenie looks smug.

Then, as quickly as they can, they hurry back to House Four.

CHAPTER FIVE
Hands

♫

"Honestly, that's the last straw," thunders Mr. Archinola when the doorbell rings at nine o'clock that night. He looks at his watch with a shake of the head. Then he squares his shoulders and strides to the door. When he opens it, at first he can see nothing in the semidarkness. But then he looks down and sees a tiny girl. She's holding a bunch of daffodils out towards him.

"Here!" she pipes.

Out of the darkness behind her steps a gigantic figure. "I'm Ben Cherry," he says, introducing himself and, at the same time, pushing a boy out in front of him.

Mr. Archinola briefly and somewhat ungraciously shakes Ben's outstretched hand. "I was expecting you at three o'clock," he says, "no earlier and no later. And certainly not at 9 p.m. I've got things to do. And so if you'll excuse me—"

The man swiftly interrupts him. "We're really, really sorry, but there were some unexpected difficulties which prevented us from getting here on time."

"Here!" pipes the little girl and once again holds out the bunch of daffodils toward Mr. Archinola. "Darry was locked in, and I'm the one who set him free!" she adds proudly. "It was that stupid Max who shut him in..."

"Be quiet, Queenie!" whispers the boy with a helpless flap of his hands.

At this moment, Mr. Archinola sees the boy's hands, motionless and frozen in the air, as if on a photograph. He is astonished. *These hands*, he thinks, *look almost exactly like my own when I was a child. I often used to look at them and wonder if I might be able to use them to make violins.*

Mr. Archinola feels like someone under a bell jar. Inside it is himself and…yes, this boy is next to him!

What's the matter with me? he asks himself, irritated. The bell jar dissolves into thin air. Uneasily, he decides. *I'll say good-bye to them, shut the door tight, turn around, and go back into the workshop. Hands or no hands, this kid has kept me dangling all day long and has stopped me from working.*

But then, as if he were made of two Archibalds, one of whom thinks and the other speaks, he clears his throat. "Archibald Archinola, master violin-maker," he hears himself say and puts out one large hand towards the boy.

The boy takes hold of it timidly. His own, much smaller hand is ice-cold.

Ben gives him a nudge. "Tell him your name!" he murmurs.

"Darius Dorian," whispers Darius.

He suddenly goes as white as chalk and closes his eyes. But before he actually falls down on the mat outside Mr. Archinola's front door, the violin-maker seizes him under the arms, picks him up, carries him to the thickly carpeted guest room, and lays him down on a felt-covered sofa.

"It's all been a bit too much for Darius today," Ben says quietly to Mr. Archinola. "Don't worry, all he needs is a good night's sleep, and then he'll be perfectly okay."

"I see," mumbles Mr. Archinola, who still finds it all very confusing.

♪ ♪ ♪ ♪ ♪ ♪

Throughout the night, Darius tosses and turns. When he opens his eyes, everything around him is unfamiliar. The light from the street lamp outside throws the cross-shaped shadows of the two huge window frames onto the ceiling and the walls of the room. Between them are the trembling shadows of leaves from a tree. Darius dreams. In his dream, a large bearded man is sitting beside him, holding his hand. Darius can feel that there is something special about the man's hand. It's strong and warm. He feels its warmth and strength flowing into his own hand, then climbing up his arm and gradually spreading through his whole body, like a light illuminating a pitch-dark room. The impressive-looking bearded man does not say a word. He simply sits there holding Darius's hand, as if at this moment there were nothing more important in the world.

The dawn breaks.

A nightingale sings its song loud and clear, and then lots of other birds join in a chorus of wild twittering.

Darius lies there, wide awake. He feels good.

Outside the window, the roof of the church is glowing green with moss.

♪ ♪ ♪ ♪ ♪ ♪

The next morning, Mr. Archinola is still so drunk with sleep that at first he doesn't even remember what happened last night. He lets out a loud yawn and switches on the crystal chandelier above the wooden table in the kitchen.

Then he hears a noise from the guest room. To be more precise, what he hears is music. Very soft and somehow muted, like a sort of miniature orchestra playing in a saucepan with the lid on. He quickly creeps to the door and puts his ear up against it.

Antonín Dvořák! Not bad at all—in fact, the very beautiful Concerto for Cello and Orchestra in B Minor, Opus 104, thinks the violin-maker sleepily, creeps away again, and slides his feet into his leather shoes. He is so tired that it doesn't even occur to him to wonder *why* there is music coming from the guest room. He's about to go to The Golden Crust, his favorite café, for his indispensable morning cup of coffee. Then the thought goes through him like a flaming arrow—the boy! He'd almost forgotten the boy!

He gently knocks on the door, behind which the soft music is still playing. No answer. Mr. Archinola opens the door. His gaze falls on the felt-covered sofa. There is no sign of the boy, but instead the bedcover is towering up in the form of a tent.

"Ahem!" Mr. Archinola goes to the sofa. "This is Mr. Violin-Maker Archinola speaking to you in person!" he says, with a little cough, because he doesn't know quite how one greets a child in the morning, and a little cough actually goes with any situation.

The music suddenly stops. The tent moves. An untidy mop of curly hair pokes out from under it, and then the rest of the boy crawls out. In his hands he's holding a pretty hideous pink radio.

"Are you feeling better today?" asks Mr. Archinola, somewhat formally, and gently strokes his beard, as if there might be trouble ahead.

"Yes," replies Darius softly. "I had a fever, but that sort of thing never lasts more than a night with me."

"Ah, right, okay then, we can go and have some breakfast," says Mr. Archinola and makes as if to leave. Then he turns around again. "What were you listening to just now?"

"I don't know," says Darius, shrugging his shoulders. "Music." He looks up and suddenly smiles. "Beautiful music."

"Do you like music?" asks the violin-maker, looking curiously at the boy.

And without hesitation, Darius answers, "Yes!"

CHAPTER SIX
Schubert and Extra Cream

♫

What Ulrich Needham likes best about his new job is the breaks, which he can spend in The Golden Crust. That is the bakery and café around the corner from his spanking new doctor's office, on St. Matthew's Square. At the café you can get cream puffs, doughnuts, miniature puddings and cakes to die for, not to mention famous people to gawk at, like actors who everybody knows from TV. And he finds *that* a thousand times more interesting than all those awful sick people who, for the last two weeks, have been boring him to death with their daily tales of stinking feet and diarrhea.

Hardly has the man with the thin fair hair sat down at a table outside, from where he has a splendid view of St. Matthew's Square, when he hears the voice of his mother.

"Ulli!" she rasps, although she's still at least a hundred yards away from The Golden Crust and her clattering heels won't carry her as far as her son for ages yet. "Ulli! Bunny, darling!"

Ulrich is so embarrassed he could sink into the ground. The couple at the next table starts giggling. Even the waiters have difficulty hiding their laughter. He grasps his knotted tie, which suddenly seems a lot too tight. The cloudless sky is a radiant steel blue. He takes off his rimless glasses and puts on his sunglasses with reflecting lenses.

"Those glasses look *ridiculous* on you!" That's his mother, who is now getting very close. "Take them off, or I'll never speak to you again!"

Sulkily he takes his sunglasses off and puts his rimless ones back on. *This spring, with all its buds and blossoms and its endlessly twittering birds, is getting on my nerves,* he thinks to himself, blinking in the sunlight. *I've been too long in the dark. Much too long. In any case, long enough for this life. It's high time things changed.*

"Have you seen those glorious magnolias in full bloom?" asks his mother, sitting beside him and taking him by the hand. "A day for *kings*, this is. A day for *you*, Bunny!"

The waitress puts a cream puff down on the table. "With extra cream for you, sir," she says. "And a Coke. I hope you enjoy it."

"What's this, what's this?" sighs his mother, raising her eyebrows. "Think of your cholesterol!" She pats his hand. "We have a long and difficult journey ahead of us until we reach our great goal. So until then, please set others a good example! After all, you're a *medical practitioner* now!" And with the word *practitioner*, she rolls the r like an opera singer. With a gracious smile, she looks around, as if she were surrounded by admirers, and then she waves to the waitress. "For me, a glass of hot skim milk, please. With three artificial sweeteners."

"Mother," says Ulrich wearily, pushing his glasses up to the bridge of his nose, "what's this all about?"

His mother looks at him indignantly. "What's what all about?" She lets out a hacking laugh that sounds like a lawnmower.

The waitress puts a glass of milk down in front of her.

"I want you to achieve something *extraordinary*! The bad times are past." With an air of conspiracy, she leans over to him and whispers, "You know what I'm talking about." Then she continues in a normal voice. "Soon everybody will know you and respect you. You have the means to do it." She swallows a mouthful of milk, which leaves her with a little white moustache. "And no one will figure it out, because we're too…"

With shining eyes and reddened cheeks, she takes hold of his tie and fiddles with the knot.

"We're too what?" Dr. Needham wants to know.

His mother doesn't answer and lets her gaze wander, as if at random, around St. Matthew's Square. "Oh, look who's coming!"

With a sugar-sweet smile, she waves to the man in the billowing coat who is just crossing the road. Behind him is a boy who is evidently having trouble keeping up with him.

"Master Violin-Maker Archibald Archinola! He's *famous* all over the city! I have the *greatest* admiration for him! Don't you?"

Violin music! Awful stuff! thinks Ulrich, but aloud he says, "Yes, indeed," and nods politely to the violin-maker as the latter sits down two tables away in the April sunshine. "Who's the boy with him?"

"How should I know?" snaps his mother impatiently and smiles her gracious smile in the direction of

Mr. Archinola. "Maybe an apprentice or something like that."

Ulrich Needham puts his reflecting sunglasses on again. Through them he can look at the boy, and no one will see him doing it.

His mother has now leaned across, and she calls obsequiously to Mr. Archinola, "When are you going to give another of your *legendary* musical evenings, which I've heard *so* much about?"

Ulrich watches the violin-maker say a few words to the boy before he comes across to their table. He gives a little bow.

"I'd be delighted to welcome you as my guests at my next Sunday concert," he says to them in the friendliest of tones. Then he turns to Ulrich. "I hear you've recently opened an office around the corner from here. You have my very best wishes for its success."

"Oh, that's right. My son is such a gifted doctor!" cries Mrs. Needham and pats her son's hand, which is lying limply on the table. "And how charming of you to invite us. And what will you be performing for us, if I may ask?"

Mr. Archinola smiles. "Schubert's String Quartet in G Major." He takes a card out of his jacket and puts it down beside Mrs. Needham's glass of milk. "Here's your invitation. Do you like Schubert?"

"Oh, how could one not like Schubert?" trills Mrs. Needham, kicking her son under the table.

"I…um…like him…too," stutters Ulrich. The fact is, he doesn't know the first thing about Schubert. He gives his shin a furtive rub.

"Then I shall look forward to seeing you soon at my place." Mr. Archinola bows again and returns to his table.

"*Those* are important people, my son," gushes Ulrich's mother and looks almost lovingly across at the violin-maker. Lost in her thoughts, she tears off a corner of the invitation card. "*That's* the sort of person you must get to know." She is shocked to see the torn piece of paper and hurriedly stuffs the two bits into her purse.

"Old habits die hard, eh, Mother?" says Ulrich with a snicker. "You'll have to wean yourself of that one."

His mother irritably reaches for her lipstick. Ulrich bites into his cream puff, and the cream oozes out of both sides and sticks to his cheeks below his sunglasses.

CHAPTER SEVEN
The Old Cabinet

🎵

The Work People Do. Three Job Shadowing Weeks with Violin-Maker Archinola, writes Darius in his notebook and uses a ruler to underline it.

The old walnut desk at which he's sitting stands in the workshop between two large open windows that look out over St. Matthew's Square. It's now afternoon, and in the distance one can hear the noises from a construction site. In the plane tree, a blackbird is chirping an intoxicated song of spring.

Although he's already been here for two days, and has talked with Mr. Archinola and watched him at work, Darius is still in a state of amazement. He swivels on the office chair. The violin-maker is standing at the workbench in his blue apron.

"This is maple, you see?" says Mr. Archinola as he hammers at an almost white piece of wood in a clamp. "It's particularly hard. Because violins are meant to last a long time, you understand? There are some that are over three hundred years old, and people are still playing them! Can you imagine that?" There's a soft rattling noise as he cuts into the wood. "The famous violin-maker Stradivarius learned from a woodcutter in the forest that some trees have such wonderful wood that it's as if they were created for the sound of the violin." He blows on the wood, and the shavings fly through the air, do a little dance with the grains of the dust in the sunlight, and then flutter to the floor. "It's even important to know whether it rained the day before the tree was cut down and if there was a full moon."

People use magic to make violins out of certain trees, writes Darius in his notebook.

He really likes the violin-maker. Mr. Archinola may not be a giant like Ben, but he is one all the same, in his own way. Because he makes violins. Because he is *able* to make violins!

The doorbell rings.

Mr. Archinola puts his chisel down on the workbench. "Hold on a second."

He goes out into the hall. A minute later, he returns. Behind him, a girl enters the workshop.

Darius doesn't know why, but for a moment he catches his breath. The girl has straight black hair that shines like polish, and the outer corners of her eyes bend upwards like the corners of a smiling mouth.

"This is Mey-Mey," says Mr. Archinola, introducing the girl. "She's twelve, just like you. And this is Darius," he says, beckoning to Mey-Mey. "He's studying the secrets of violin-making."

The children nod to each other. *This girl,* thinks Darius to himself, *has eyes like two lakes with not even the tiniest wave.*

"May I?" she asks, pointing to the room behind the open double door. Mr. Archinola calls it his "salesroom."

"Carry on," he says.

Darius watches the girl as she walks across the room. There is a cello leaning against a music stand with an open score. In the middle of the floor is a wooden chair with blue upholstery and curved legs. And in an old display cabinet, reddish, yellowish, and brownish violins hang by their scrolls. This is where Mr. Archinola keeps his collection of violins that nobody wants—like those he has found at flea markets or some that have been given to him to repair but have never been reclaimed. One day, he says, when he's very old, he will take a closer look at them all and will restore their varnish.

When Darius's gaze wanders over the glass doors of this cabinet, he suddenly sees something strange. There's a blue light—no doubt about it—coming from one of the violins! To be precise, it's the second one on the left. He blinks rapidly three or four times. The blue light is still there! In fact, the glow is getting even brighter, almost like a sunbeam. Has Mr. Archinola seen it too? Darius squints across at the violin-maker, but he's completely absorbed in his work again. Darius shakes his head like a wet dog trying to get the drops out of his coat, and then he looks at the violin again. But the light has disappeared.

Only now does he see that Mey-Mey is kneeling over a violin case on the floor. The clasps click as she opens it. Carefully she takes out a violin and bow.

"Mey-Mey hasn't got a violin of her own," whispers Mr. Archinola. "Her parents aren't too keen on this passion of hers. That's why she often comes here to practice."

The girl strokes the strings of the bow with a little stone of yellow glass.

"She doesn't even go to the swimming pool or the movies or buy herself an ice cream—she prefers to play the violin," says Mr. Archinola, and it sounds as if he's really proud of Mey-Mey. Then he lets out a sigh. "But she's got this problem."

"What sort of problem?" asks Darius curiously.

"Well," whispers Mr. Archinola, pointing his iron file in Mey-Mey's direction, "just look closely. She's got a stiff left forefinger. That's not good for a violinist, as I'm sure you can imagine."

He starts filing. The jars, brushes, and chisels on the workbench shake to the rhythm of his filing. Inside a corked bottle, something liquid wobbles up and down like a tiny ocean in a tiny storm.

"But *can* she play or not?" persists Darius, looking surprised, as Mey-Mey has just placed the violin against her shoulder. Now he can see that her left forefinger is sticking up in the air, while the rest of her fingers are on the strings.

"Oh yes," says Mr. Archinola, nodding. "And she's good too. But grass doesn't grow under the competition, if you know what I mean. That stiff finger has closed a lot of doors to her. Five flexible fingers are better than four—at least that's the way people think in the musical world. Yes, indeed, it's a real shame."

From the salesroom a melody now wings its way into the workshop. Clear and warm.

Darius lays his pen on one side, leans back, and folds his hands behind his head. The melody slides deep into his body. It's beautiful. It's a thousand times more beautiful than with the pink radio under the sheets. He closes his eyes. And although his eyes are closed, he can see something wonderful: the workshop doesn't have an ornate ceiling as it did before. Suddenly there's a flock of birds—white, light brown, and silver. Darius can see the sky above him, and the birds soaring up into a vast, bright expanse of blue. So freely do they fly into this blue that Darius follows them, higher and higher. And up there, in the midst of the music and the blue, suddenly all other sounds have faded away. There is silence. A bright, total silence…

Darius gives a start.

Mey-Mey is standing beside him. It seems that she's just asked him something.

"S-Sorry?" stammers Darius. With difficulty he returns from the distant blue to the wooden floor of the workshop. The music seems to have ended long ago.

"Are you writing a poem?" she asks, looking inquisitively at his notebook, which is lying there open.

Darius notices a brown stain on her neck. Then he stares at the last sentence in his notebook: *The violins make me disappear into heaven.*

He can't remember writing it. He feels awkward. In embarrassment, he covers the sentence with his hand.

"You're good at it," he says quickly, and when she gives him a puzzled look, he adds, "Playing the violin."

He's surprised at his own boldness. After all, Mey-Mey's a girl, and what's more, she's a complete stranger.

She immediately goes red. "But I have to practice quite a lot," she says and awkwardly raises her hand to the brown patch on her neck.

"You're bound to become famous!" says Darius. He doesn't even think of her stiff forefinger.

"Hm," she murmurs, shrugging her shoulders. She points to Darius's jacket, which is hanging over the back of the chair. "By the way, I like that lovely old jacket of yours."

"Thanks," he says, somewhat surprised, because apart from himself, nobody likes his old jacket.

Mey-Mey puts her palms together, as if in prayer, and makes a little bow to Mr. Archinola. "Thank you for letting me practice here," she says, very seriously.

Then she turns once more to Darius. "Will we meet again at the musical evening?"

Darius's heart suddenly starts beating faster. With some difficulty he manages a lighthearted "Maybe."

"That would be nice." Once again she puts her hands together and gives him a little bow as well. "Because with Schubert, too, it's quite easy to disappear into heaven," she says.

Then suddenly she's gone.

The door to Mr. Archinola's apartment closes softly.

Darius can't help himself. He stands up and goes to the open window. He positions himself so that he can quickly jump to the side if Mey-Mey should look up. But to his surprise, he sees a man and a woman in St. Matthew's Square, and they're having an animated discussion just a few yards away from the front door of the house. Isn't that the new doctor—what's his name? Needham?—and his mother? Instinctively, Darius pulls his head back inside and listens to the angry but muted voice of the man.

"Don't be such a damned worrywart, Mother! You're beginning to make me nervous! No one's going to figure out the fact that I—"

The front door slams shut and drowns the rest of his sentence in the thunderclap. Darius peeps out of the window again. When Mey-Mey suddenly appears and looks up at him, he can't draw back quickly enough. Their eyes meet. He raises his hand and waves. Mey-Mey smiles, waves back, and then disappears from view.

"Fiddle-di-dee, I need to go to the post office!" says Mr. Archinola, and Darius is forced to return his body and mind to the workshop. "It won't take long, boy. Can I leave you alone for a quarter of an hour?"

"Of course," replies Darius.

"As soon as I come back, I'll let you do some work with the chisel!" the violin-maker calls out.

When the door to the apartment closes for a second time, everything is quiet. Darius bends over his notebook. But then he takes a sideways look into the salesroom. And once again he lets his gaze wander almost randomly over the glass doors of the cabinet. It must have been an optical illusion before, when the violin…glowed. Glowed blue. Darius shakes his head, like Ben calling for a bit of common sense, but at this precise moment once again, there is a glow in the cabinet. Blue. And this time it doesn't stop glowing, not even when he blinks a few times, shakes his head, and looks elsewhere, as if the cabinet and everything in it were not of the slightest interest.

Darius's heart again beats faster. He puts his pen down and stands up.

CHAPTER EIGHT
No Cut

I t seems like an age before Darius reaches the cabinet. And yet all he has to do is walk across two large rooms. The sun is shining through onto his right cheek, the cello, the chair with bent legs, and the violin case that is lying on the floor, as if abandoned. The sun makes the glass doors of the cabinet, before which he is now standing, sparkle and flash.

It's so bright I can't see a thing, he says to himself and pulls the brass handle on one of the doors. It's locked.

He opens the top drawer and finds a lot of little tins and wooden boxes in it. He opens some of them. They contain amber-colored stones that smell of incense. It's rosin. But where is the key to the cabinet?

Darius pulls the drawer a bit farther out, and in the back left-hand corner he finds a little yellow cloth like those used to clean glasses with. He lifts it up. Beneath it is a brass key, old and tarnished. Darius picks it up and puts it in the lock. He turns it. With a little creak, the cabinet door opens. As if awakening from a long sleep, the violins rock on their scrolls, click against each other, and of their own accord let out softly vibrating sounds. Into his nostrils wafts a smell of dust and wood that was once moist but is now quite dry.

Hm, nothing at all glowing here, thinks Darius. But he knows exactly which violin it was that had given off that strange blue light a few moments ago. Resolutely, he takes the second violin on the left from its support.

A thought suddenly occurs to him. *If Mr. Archinola should catch me now, he'll think I'm trying to steal something. Only I just want to have a closer look at this violin.*

He hastily sticks it under his arm and closes the cabinet door. *Oh no, now you can see a gap!* With trembling fingers, he opens the door again and arranges all the violins so that they're the same distance from one another. Then once more he closes the door.

No one'll notice now, he thinks to himself with relief.

As he puts the brass key back under the yellow cloth, he hears the heavy footsteps of Mr. Archinola coming up the stairs. He quickly closes the drawer, hurries into the guest room, and hides the violin under the sofa.

♪ ♪ ♪ ♪ ♪ ♪

"Ouch!"

Soon afterward Darius is standing at the workbench. He lets go of the handle of the chisel, and with a loud clatter, the tool falls onto the wooden floor. Shocked, he sticks his left forefinger in his mouth. He grimaces and sniffs. There's a taste of metal.

"Oh, good Lord!" cries Mr. Archinola and hurries across to the medicine cabinet. He pulls open a drawer marked Clips and Clasps, rummages around, and comes back with a white bandage. "Let's see."

Darius holds his finger out to the violin-maker. It's bleeding quite heavily.

"That's gone pretty deep!" Mr. Archinola clicks his tongue with annoyance. "I should never have let you work with something as sharp as that!" He winds the bandage around Darius's finger. "Is it very painful?"

Darius nods. It certainly is. Max's forefinger digging between his ribs is nothing compared to this. And what a fool he's made of himself! Clumsy oaf! Now Mr. Archinola will think he's totally incompetent—that's obvious.

His finger is starting to throb.

"We must keep an eye on that cut," says Mr. Archinola, tapping the workbench with his knuckles. "If it gets inflamed, we'll go and see the doctor. Maybe the new one here in St. Matthew's. What's his name again? Oh yes, Needham." He sweeps a few wood shavings off the workbench and throws them in the bin.

Darius doesn't know why, but at the moment when Mr. Archinola says the name of the doctor, the cut starts to burn like fire.

♪ ♪ ♪ ♪ ♪ ♪ ♪

In the middle of the night, Darius wakes up. He hears footsteps clattering across St. Matthew's Square, coming nearer, and then fading into the distance. The wind is rustling through the plane tree, and a branch knocks against the window. Darius looks at the cross-shaped pattern of the window on the ceiling. Inside it, the shadows of the leaves are waving and trembling, just as they did on his first night. But tonight he doesn't have a fever. There is something else keeping him awake.

Silently, he slides off the sofa and sits cross-legged on the carpet. His finger is still throbbing. Gently he pulls the violin out from under the sofa. Its thin, light wood creaks in his hands, and its strings let out a soft sound.

"Now what's the matter with you?" he whispers to himself.

He turns the violin round and round. "You're beautiful, that's for sure." Then he runs his good forefinger around the curved f-holes to the right and left of the strings. He raises the violin in front of his face and holds the openings close to his eye. Too dark. He reaches for his jeans, and from one pocket he fishes out a little flashlight. He switches it on with a click, shines it into one of the narrow holes, very slowly turns the violin around, and peers through the slit. There! He can definitely see something! A little yellowed sign stuck on the wood. Darius has to move the violin away from his eye for a moment, because everything is blurred. He takes a deep breath and then looks inside again.

"Pizz...ica...to. One...six...nine...two," he reads. "Sixteen-ninety-two, Pizzicato." He lowers the violin and looks out of the window. The first light of morning is brushing against the moss on the church roof. A nightingale sings. Maybe the violin was made in 1692, but what's the meaning of "Pizzicato"? Darius holds the violin tenderly on his lap. It looks as if the neck had been broken at some time. At least there's a fine line like a crack. For a moment he lightly plucks the strings.

This thick bandage is a nuisance, he thinks to himself. *I can't hold the violin properly.*

He quickly unwinds the white gauze from his finger. The wound is wide and deep.

Darius goes on plucking the strings. He does it very softly, so as not to wake Mr. Archinola. *I mustn't say anything till I know what's so strange about this violin,* he thinks. Somehow, these soft notes remind him of Mey-Mey. How she moves her head. How she walks. How she speaks.

Darius plucks. And at the same time, he feels the pain in his finger getting stronger and stronger, and it's throbbing like mad.

Shoot, I must put the bandage back on, he says miserably to himself.

He's just about to stop plucking the strings when, all at once, the terrible pain disappears.

"Now what's happening?" he asks.

He takes his hand away from the violin and stares at his finger. There is no cut to be seen. "It must have…It can only have been my right forefinger then!" he mumbles in confusion. Then he looks at it in bewilderment. No cut. His heart pounds. Now he examines all his fingers, one by one, and turns his hands this way and that.

There is no cut.

CHAPTER NINE
Everyone's In a Hurry

♪

"Did you sleep well, boy? You look so…so…Somehow you look different from yesterday," muses Mr. Archinola the next morning as Darius comes from his room into the kitchen.

Darius looks at the floor. "No, I mean, yes, I slept very well," he says quickly.

The truth is, he didn't get a wink after his strange adventure with Pizzicato. Almost all night long, he looked at the violin, touched it, and carried it around the room like a sleeping baby. And again and again he stared in disbelief at his finger, which after several hours still looked perfectly normal, with not even a scratch.

"So how's the cut? Let's have a look." Mr. Archinola comes across to see it.

"I've just looked at it myself and put the bandage back on," Darius says hastily and holds up his bandaged finger as if to prove it. "But it hardly hurts at all now."

Mr. Archinola furrows his brow. "Well, all right, if you're happy with it. We'll look at it again tomorrow morning."

Suddenly he puts his arm around Darius's shoulders. Darius is so pleased that he scarcely dares to breathe. It's as if his shoulders were now made of porcelain. He tries to keep his porcelain shoulders from moving under the warm, heavy arm of Mr. Archinola.

"Please can I help you again today?" he asks, holding up his injured finger. "In spite of this?"

The violin-maker says nothing for a while.

The "while" lasts long enough for Darius to start thinking about Pizzicato again. *I must find out as quickly as possible what's special about it,* he resolves. *Otherwise, I'll begin to believe I've gone crazy. I'd better not tell Mr. Archinola yet, or he'll think so too! No way must he realize there's anything strange going on.*

"Today I'm going to show you how to string a bow," Mr. Archinola says, finally breaking the silence. "It's Mr. Kaplan's—he plays the viola in our quartet. It's got to be ready by tomorrow." He clears his throat. "Because if you're going to be a violin-maker, you must also learn how to string a bow."

You need about two hundred horse hairs for a bow. They are secured by the so-called frog with the help of a little block of wood, writes Darius. His writing is a bit more shaky than yesterday, because he keeps thinking about Pizzicato and his healed finger underneath the bandage. He himself is a bit shaky too, because he really hates having to lie. And he will have to lie to Mr. Archinola today, even though he likes the violin-maker more and more with every hour that passes.

He goes to join Mr. Archinola at the workbench. "Without a good bow," says the violin-maker cheerfully, "even the best Stradivarius doesn't sound right." He holds a thick bundle of white threads, each as long as an arm, out in front of Darius's nose. "My bow hairs are from the tails of Mongolian horses, drawn three times. They're tied double and knotted three times. They last incredibly well."

He has put Mr. Kaplan's bow in a screw clamp, and now he tests it with his fingers.

"When you've done your work properly, the bow feels wonderfully springy, and it sits so comfortably in the hand that violinists can make their instruments sing with the sound they've been dreaming of," he says enthusiastically. With his left hand he's holding the white horse hairs firmly over the block of wood, and with his right he runs a comb along them. "Try it," he tells Darius, then steps aside and hands him the black comb.

Darius stands in front of the clamped bow. He's nervous, just as he is every time Mr. Archinola lets him try something.

Slowly he strokes the hairs with the comb. There's a gentle chirping noise as he does it, and it blends with the song of the blackbird from outside. He combs over and over again, slowly and carefully. He wishes he could take the bandage off his finger, but then Mr. Archinola would see that the wound has already healed! *You and an Australian wombat would really make a fine couple!* He can suddenly hear Mrs. Helmet's sneering voice in his head. He's shocked and immediately stops combing. *They get run over because they're so slow!* The voice jangles on. The mocking laughter of his classmates sounds as real as if they were all sitting right behind him here in the workshop.

Humiliated, he lets the hand with the comb drop to his side. *I'm just a stupid slugboy,* he thinks. *They're right, and that's it.*

"Not bad, boy." Mr. Archinola breaks in on his thoughts. He nods his approval and strokes the bow hairs with his fingers. Then he murmurs softly, "Not bad at all—in fact, pretty good!"

He looks at Darius with interest, as if this were the first time they'd met. "Okay, let me try again now," he says.

Darius is pleasantly surprised and makes way.

"You've got a rare tranquillity in those hands of yours," says Mr. Archinola. "That's important for violin-making." He pauses. "Everyone's in a hurry today! It's all one long rush! So how are good violins made, eh? Good violins aren't made—how shall I put it?—with a whoosh! And certainly not with all these modern…adding machines!" Now he sounds almost angry.

"You mean computers?" asks Darius.

"Yes, these modern gadgets," grumbles the violin-maker.

For a while the two of them remain silent. Darius watches Mr. Archinola very closely, and his movements imprint themselves on the boy's memory. He's hugely delighted that the violin-maker praised him. But that makes it all the worse that he will soon have to lie to him.

"Is Mey-Mey coming today?" he finally asks. He would like to hear her music again and see the silver birds in the wide blue sky. And her.

Since she was at the workshop, he can't help thinking about her sometimes. In fact—often. Well actually, he thinks about her nearly all the time.

"No, she won't come till Sunday after next, for the soirée. She still needs to practice her *pizzicato* and *martellato*—those are her biggest weaknesses," murmurs Mr. Archinola, as if lost in his own thoughts.

Darius starts. *Practice her pizzicato?* He gulps. *Pizzicato 1692,* he thinks to himself.

"What…What does pizzicato actually mean?" he asks as casually as possible.

"Well, it's one of many ways of playing the strings," explains Mr. Archinola, loosening the clamp. "When you see the word on the score, it means you have to pluck the strings instead of bowing them."

He takes out the bow and looks at it with an expression of satisfaction.

"I see," says Darius with exaggerated calm, though his thoughts are galloping around his head like startled horses after a pistol shot. If what he's slowly beginning to suspect is actually true, and if the violin under the felt-covered sofa can do what he thinks it can do, then maybe…no, surely, he'll be able to help Mey-Mey!

CHAPTER TEN

Rags and a Gold Mine

♫

Next morning, endless lines of cars drive past Darius, and in the sidewalk cafés people are sitting in their sunglasses behind their newspapers, as if they're all from the crime squad and are keeping watch on him. This early in the morning, it's still quite chilly. In one hand Darius has his duffel bag. It's light, because there's nothing in it except Pizzicato.

Mr. Archinola thinks Darius has to go to school today in order to discuss his project. Darius is deeply ashamed at having made up such a cock-and-bull story, but he *has* to find out what's so special about this Pizzicato. And there's one thing above all that he wants: to help Mey-Mey and her violin playing so that no musical door will ever be closed to her again. Because he knows how well she can play! He's never seen silver birds before, and he's never been able to fly! Mey-Mey is a sorceress when she plays the violin, that's for sure.

He stops in a large cobbled square. A jackhammer is making an unholy racket, and there are pigeons pecking at crumbs on the ground. Underneath a lime tree with yellow-green buds is a bench on which a woman is sitting. Next to her stands a shopping cart, and in it are piles of plastic bags, newspapers, and a dirty gray blanket. These seem to be her only possessions.

Okay, thinks Darius, *this is where we start.*

He goes to the bench and sits down. The old woman doesn't look at him. She's busy. She takes a slice of bread from a package, and then she pours something out of a thermos into a cup. White steam rises up into the cold, sunny morning air. Darius looks sideways at the woman's leg. There are some rags tied around her calf. The foot poking out underneath is covered with scratches.

"That's right, sonny," says the woman, who has noticed him looking. "That's what 'appens when ya live on the streets like me. It's always the same."

She seems nice. She bites into her bread and chews it noisily.

"Does it hurt?" asks Darius.

"Course it 'urts," says the woman and stretches out her leg as if that would help Darius understand exactly how much it hurts. "But what you wanna know that for?" She slurps her drink from her cup. "Not your problem."

Darius carefully lifts Pizzicato out of his duffel bag and lays it on his lap. He's concentrating so hard on what he's about to do that he sees nothing except the violin and the woman chewing her bread. If he were to look up and straight ahead, he would see Mrs. Needham come out of a shop with an armful of white coats, stop with a jerk, and then squint her eyes and fix them firmly on him.

"What'cha gonna do with that?" asks the woman in surprise. "Gonna collect some money fer me an' my poor leg?"

Darius doesn't answer. As if at random, he begins to pluck the strings. Some chickadees in the lime tree over the bench start twittering. Darius goes on plucking. At first the sounds are uncoordinated, but gradually his left and right forefingers get into more and more of a rhythm. A pair of white butterflies goes fluttering past.

The woman has stopped eating. She sits there listening with her eyes closed. Darius looks at her and goes on plucking the strings. He already has a good idea of what is about to happen. And then, the woman suddenly pulls a face as if someone has slapped her. Startled, she grabs hold of her bandaged calf. Darius plays on, although he feels sorry for the woman. He knows that this is precisely how it has to be.

All at once the woman lets go of her leg, and Darius stops plucking the strings. The last notes fade away. The woman says nothing. Then she looks at her foot. Bewildered, she twists and turns it. There is not a scratch to be seen. With an expression almost of fear, she looks at Darius. Slowly she unwraps the gray rags around her calf. The leg beneath is completely healed.

"What'cha gone an' done to me, sonny?" she whispers. She reaches for Darius's hand and grasps it tightly. "How didja do it?"

Darius puts the violin back in his duffel bag. He presses the woman's hand and slowly gets up. He is happy that the woman's cuts and scratches have disappeared.

It really looks as if everything he had suspected is true: with Pizzicato he can heal people. But he wants to be quite certain before he tells Mey-Mey and gets her hopes up.

"All the best," he says softly. "I have to go now."

Even now, Darius does not notice Mrs. Needham, who in the meantime has hidden behind a tree and is watching intently.

When he disappears down the next side street, she scurries after him, like a lizard hunting a tasty grasshopper.

♪ ♪ ♪ ♪ ♪ ♪ ♪

"Excuse me, Doctor, but your mother insists on seeing you!" stammers Angelica, the receptionist, as she stands red-faced in the doorway of Ulrich Needham's consultation room.

"*Will* you let me through, for heaven's sake!" screeches Mrs. Needham indignantly and pushes the girl aside. "Bunny, I must speak with you, *now!*"

She carelessly tosses the white coats onto a chair, flounces across to the desk, and sits down. She clasps her purse tightly on her lap. Her hair is sticking up from her head in a somewhat unusual confusion.

"Mother, I've told you a hundred times not to disturb me during my office hours!" hisses Ulrich, waving the receptionist away. He once heard a doctor say this on a TV show, and he had been extremely impressed. In actual fact, though, he doesn't mind at all if he's kept away from his tedious duties.

"*Is that how you speak to your mother?*" she shrieks.

Ulrich jerks his head back and then watches his mother take a mirror and comb out of her purse and straighten her hair. When she's satisfied, she continues in a whisper, "I've seen *him* again!" Her voice quakes, and she squints nervously at her son.

"Seen who again?"

She gives a scornful snort. "The boy, for heaven's sake! The snail of a lad who the violin-maker has had in tow for the last couple of days. But you'll never believe what I've just seen, Bunny! He's an absolute *gold mine!*"

"Gold mine? How come?" asks Ulrich in disbelief.

"For heaven's sake, Bunny, close your practice now! I'll explain later! We're as good as made!"

Ulrich jerks his head forward. He swiftly presses a button on his telephone, fixing his watery eyes on his mother.

"Under no circumstances am I to be disturbed for the next hour," he says curtly into the speaker. "Oh, what the hell, close the practice for the rest of the day and send all the patients home."

He and his mother now have their tête-à-tête, and what Ulrich hears leaves him with his mouth wide open. The more his mother tells him about the miracles she saw as she followed the boy through the town, the darker glows the expression of greed in his eyes.

CHAPTER ELEVEN

Cremona

O n Friday afternoon, Alice Ponticello is sitting with her mother and Uncle Adriano in Ebbli's Coffee House, right in the center of the old part of Cremona. It's very warm, as it has been for days all over Italy. There's a giant fan slowly revolving on the ceiling. Baroque music is playing quietly through the speakers, and people are talking and laughing.

"Three double espressos, three *pan* Cremoneses, and three *torrones!*" orders Uncle Adriano.

"But Uncle Adriano, it's only a week ago that Mama had a heart attack!" whispers Alice. "And then the tiring journey here. She shouldn't be having so many rich cakes and coffee."

"Nonsense!" thunders her uncle merrily and lays his big, hairy hand on the shoulder of Alice's mother, who gives it a cheerful pat. "Your mama had a heart attack simply because she was missing *me*—that's all!" He roars with laughter, and Alice's mother giggles. "In any case, it's marvelous that the two of you have come to see me after all this time, eh? You were four years old and wearing pigtails last time I saw you, Alice. I don't suppose you'll even remember the city. Ah, Cremona, the city of violins—always worth a visit!" he says enthusiastically.

With a clatter, the waiter puts the plates and cups down in front of them.

"Cremona's the city of violins?" asks Alice. "I didn't know that! My best friend is a violin-maker," she says, digging into her torrone.

"Ah, then this is where he'd certainly find his true friends," comments Uncle Adriano with his mouth full. "Because we've got the biggest violin-making school in the whole world! Young people come here from as far as Japan and America just to learn this famous craft from us." It sounds almost as if Uncle Adriano had set up the violin-making school with his own hands, he's that proud of it.

When the three of them are so full of sweets that they can scarcely utter another word, Uncle Adriano puts his napkin to one side and says, "If you feel like it, I'll show you the violin museum in the Palazzo Comunale—our city hall. There you'll hear a very mysterious tale about a violin which the music world is still puzzling over."

He puts some money on the table, stands up, and offers his arm to Alice's mother. She hooks her arm in and cuddles up close to him.

"So what sort of mystery is this?" asks Alice with sudden curiosity, and she hooks herself onto her uncle's other arm.

He winks at her. "Just come with me."

The three of them leave the via Cavalotti Felice and soon find themselves in the via Robolotti.

"This is the street where many of the violin-makers have their workshops, as you can even see from the outside," says Uncle Adriano, pointing to the houses, which all look medieval.

It's true. Out of one house after another, Alice can now hear the sawing, hammering, and planing. The sounds of violins playing also waft through the air. Suddenly Alice feels homesick. *Oh, Archie,* she thinks, *I miss you. If only you knew how much!*

At last they come to the city hall. The great colonnaded arcades at the front and the little crenellations on the roof make it look like a rather flat castle.

"Let's go in," says Uncle Adriano, opening the front door. "I'll take you to the *saletta dei violini,* if Signor Mosconi gives us permission." He looks around. "He's the museum curator and happens to be a friend of mine. And believe it or not, every day he plays all the Stradivariuses himself, just so they don't lose their magic tone! Ah, there he is!"

Uncle Adriano greets an elderly, gray-haired man with a hearty slap on the back, and the small, fragile-looking gentleman looks as if he's going to need at least two days to recover from it. The two of them have a quick conversation, and just a few minutes later, Uncle Adriano and his guests are standing in a lofty room, on whose walls are huge, resplendent mirrors with ornate gold frames. Hanging in countless glass cubes are the violins. They look as if they're hovering in midair behind the glass.

"And now have a look at this," says Uncle Adriano as they go to the far corner of the room.

They are confronted by a glass cube on a socle that looks no different from all the others.

Except that it's empty.

Alice steps closer and deciphers the writing on a small sign that's fixed to the floor.

PIZZICATO 1692. DISAPPEARED.
REAPPEARED IN 1753.
DISAPPEARED.
REAPPEARED IN 1834.
DISAPPEARED.
HAS NOT BEEN SEEN SINCE.

"So what's that all about?" asks Alice curiously.

"Yes, Adriano, tell us about it," says Alice's mother with equal interest as she puts her reading glasses back in her purse.

"Well," says Uncle Adriano, "it's the strange tale of the so-called magic violin of Cremona. The story goes that its neck was broken, and it was repaired in 1692 by none other than Stradivarius himself. Since it was repaired by the great maestro—or you might say it was healed—it's believed to have developed healing powers of its own. They say that anyone who plucked its strings was able to cure illnesses of all kinds on the spot." Thoughtfully he strokes his chin and gazes at the empty glass cube. "Since then, at irregular intervals, it keeps on turning up out of the blue, but then each time it seems to disappear again! Anyway, it's been gone for such a long time now that no sensible person can believe in such a fairy tale. So that's it. Legend has it, though, that the person who finds it will be particularly kindhearted, will have strikingly tranquil hands, and will love music. And so he'll get the chance to do good with this Pizzicato—in other words, to heal people."

Uncle Adriano pauses, as if he has to work out whether he's finished his little violin lecture or not.

"Oh yes," he says, pointing his forefinger up in the air. "If the instrument falls into the hands of someone with evil intent, its effects can be the exact opposite."

He suddenly claps his hands, and the sound echoes all around the room. "Personally," he says, "I think it's a load of nonsense. Humbug! A tourist attraction, nothing more. All this mystique about violins is just a lot of claptrap. But on the other hand, the tale has made a lot of money for Cremona over the years." He leans forward and whispers, "There are more people driving Ferraris in this city than anywhere else, if you get my meaning."

He winks at Alice and her mother, holds out his elbows, which each of them hooks onto, and the three of them leave the city hall.

CHAPTER TWELVE

Cardboard and Customers

Darius looks at the clock on St. Matthew's Church and gets a shock. It's almost six! Mr. Archinola will be worried, he thinks, and so he speeds up. Today has gone like a sort of time-lapse film. He's lost count of the number of people he's been able to heal with Pizzicato, but there were certainly lots of them. He thinks back over the list: There was the boy in the playground with a gash in his head that closed even before his father had realized he'd fallen over. Then the old man in the wheelchair who suddenly stood up and ran off while his wife collapsed with shock in the middle of the sidewalk. There was also the fruit-seller, who would have almost sliced off his fingertip cutting melons if Darius hadn't been there plucking the strings. And there was the car accident on Tindall Avenue, with three injured people who were all miraculously healed by the time the ambulance arrived with its flashing lights. The paramedics couldn't believe it when they saw the wrecked cars and realized that the people had no injuries.

Anyway, one thing is now crystal clear: this violin can heal the worst of injuries and ailments, thinks Darius. But it's all so crazy that no one will ever believe him. It doesn't matter. The main thing is that he'll be able to help Mey-Mey.

Darius looks up. The sky is now overcast, and the air has become damp and heavy. The birds' chirping has gone quiet, as if they're silently hoping for the rain that now weighs on the town like a great expectation. Darius's duffel bag seems heavier than before. In the distance he can hear a baby crying.

He's relieved to see the name Archibald Archinola—Master Violin-Maker on the metal sign, and he's just taken hold of the front door handle when he hears something. He turns around. A man is dragging himself in the direction of the church. He's wearing a strange black cape and a funny hat, even though the weather is so clammy, and his back is all bent.

Darius listens. Yes! The man is crying! No doubt about it! With great difficulty, he now pulls open the church door. One might almost think that he gives Darius an imploring look before he disappears inside.

Darius looks at his duffel bag with Pizzicato nestling in it. *Maybe it would be better if I tested its miraculous powers one last time. Better safe than sorry.*

Having made up his mind, he lets go of the door handle and hurries across St. Matthew's Square. A moment later, the door of the church closes behind him with a solemn crash.

♪ ♪ ♪ ♪ ♪

Initially, Darius has to get used to the dim light inside the church. He blinks a few times. Hideously discordant notes resound from the giant organ pipes in the upper story. He clasps the handle of his duffel bag and walks slowly past the columns and arches, which are painted with earthy red and olive green stripes, like candy. Electric lightbulbs hang down from the high ceiling over the nave, and there are flames flickering from thick white candles, as if fighting against the artificial lights.

Suddenly the organ music stops. Through the loud-speaker comes the sound of someone clearing his throat, and Darius now sees a priest standing at the altar. In a bored and grating tone, he starts to read from a thick black book, and his voice whirrs down the aisle like some tired gray moth. There's a smell of stale incense.

In one of the wooden pews at the back, a man is kneel-ing. Darius can hardly make him out under the black cape and hat. His head is lowered, his hands are folded, and he is murmuring something out loud. Darius slips softly into the pew behind him and sits down close to him. Then he cautiously looks around.

Fortunately, the church is empty apart from them. This doesn't seem to bother the priest, who simply drones on. Then he makes a sign of the cross in the air and swiftly strides out of the chancel. The jangling organ music starts up again. The man is still kneeling with low-ered head, and from time to time he lets out a sob. Poor fellow!

Now I can risk it, thinks Darius sympathetically, and he opens the zipper of his duffel bag with a *zzzzzz.* Softly he takes Pizzicato out, puts it on his lap, and gently rests his hands on its strings.

Suddenly someone seizes him from behind!

As he tries to shout for help, something damp is pressed over his mouth and nose. Helplessly he breathes in the sharp smell. For a moment, the lightbulbs, candle flames, striped columns, and organ pipes swirl before his eyes, and then everything goes black.

"All done?" asks the man in the black cape, and he turns around. On the face beneath the hat there is not the slightest sign of concern.

"Yes, help me! Hurry up!" says a woman's voice.

Both the man and the woman quickly glance around the interior of the church. When they're certain that no one is watching them, they grasp Darius by the hands and feet and dump him in a large cardboard box that is standing on the floor next to the confessional.

"Have you got the violin?" asks the man nervously.

The woman nods and holds Pizzicato up in the air.

"Then let's go!" murmurs the man.

"Now we can look at the boy's fingers, to see how he works these miracle cures." The woman snickers. "What would you do without me, Bunny?" she whispers.

♪ ♪ ♪ ♪ ♪ ♪ ♪

"One part sandarac, one part mastic, and one part lacquer." Mr. Archinola is talking aloud to himself, trying to make himself concentrate as he grinds everything together in a mortar. It's now eight o'clock…School never went on that long in his day!

The violin-maker pours the finely ground resin into bottles, adds some alcohol, and starts to shake them. Maybe Darius has gone to see his friends in the children's home. He shakes every bottle as violently as if he could force an answer out of it.

No, I've had enough of this, he thinks. He hurriedly takes the newly prepared varnish to the dark storeroom and then goes to the hall, where he anxiously hunts for the phone number of the Stork's Nest Children's Home. But when he's just about to dial the number, the phone rings. It gives Mr. Archinola a terrible shock.

"Oh fiddlesticks!" he mumbles. "I'm now a nervous wreck!"

He picks up the receiver and says, "Nervous Wreck Archinola. Oh, sorry, I mean Violin-Maker Archinola."

He puts his hand to his forehead and realizes that he's once again sweating with apprehension.

"Mr. Archinola?" says an unfamiliar voice. It sounds distant and muffled.

"Speaking," he replies.

"This is the municipal Stork's Nest Children's Home. I'm afraid we have to inform you that Darius wants to end the project with you. He's back with us. You needn't wait for him any longer."

Mr. Archinola needs a few moments to pull himself together. "You mean...the boy...he doesn't want to stay...oh!"

"You know how it is with these brats. First it's one thing; then it's another. And Darius is a particularly bad case." The caller gives a shrill laugh. "We're very sorry if he's caused you any trouble."

"Well no, he hasn't caused me any...um...Could I... Maybe I could have a word with him?" asks Mr. Archinola. "I'd like him to tell me himself what's the matter."

In the background he can hear what sounds like an argument, but he can't make out what's being said. Then finally he recognizes the boy's voice.

"Darius Dorian," it says, trembling.

"What on earth has happened, boy?" asks the violin-maker incredulously. "We were going to work together on…"

There are more angry noises, as if people are quarrelling at the other end of the line.

"I…I don't want to do it anymore," says Darius in a strangled tone. "I find violin-making…totally boring."

Before Mr. Archinola can reply, the voice of the first caller is back on the line. "Listen, there's no point in you talking to the boy. We know our customers. Darius is a hopeless case—a complete waste of time. What I call a no-hoper. No offense to you, Mr. Archinola. We're grateful to you for all your trouble. We'll fetch Darius's belongings later. Good-bye."

There is a click at the other end.

Mr. Archinola stands in the hall with the receiver in his hand and stares into empty space.

CHAPTER THIRTEEN
The Wonder Doctor

Someone is holding a cup to Darius's lips. His head is throbbing. He takes a few sips and sinks back in his bed—a thin foam mat on a gray linoleum floor.

"No, you mustn't sleep! No, no! Wake up! It's surgery time!"

The woman's shrill voice, which he has heard so often over the last few days, makes his head hurt even more.

Initially, she had just wanted Darius to "understand" why he was here. She'd said it was his duty to heal people and that would work much better through the practice of Dr. Needham, her son, than outside on the streets, where sooner or later someone would steal the violin anyway. But first, she said, he had to build up his strength, and so she'd given him food and drink and then held something under his nose that gave off fumes that made him sleep. He had dozed through the weekend, and when the patients had come flooding in on Monday, she made Darius hide behind the white curtain in the examination room. He must always start plucking the strings of the violin when Dr. Needham gave him the signal. Right from the start, Darius disliked Dr. Needham. At some time or other, this pale-faced smart-ass, with his bespectacled, watery, piggy little eyes, would say the following to his patients: *"I'm now going to perform a miracle on you. Please have faith in my unique magic powers. Close your eyes."*

That was the cue for Darius to pluck the strings of Pizzicato behind the curtain. The woman sat right next to him the whole time, watching his hands. And she sat there with the soaked ball of cotton in her hand. If he were to let out just a cry for help or were to risk trying to run away, she had warned him that she would press the pad under his nose. And then they would *"quietly dispose of him."* Darius believed her. This was not a woman to mess with. She was at least as bad as her would-be doctor son.

Darius takes a deep breath.

How on earth can I get out of here? he asks himself feverishly, putting Pizzicato on his lap. *Worst of all, this Needham wants to start playing Pizzicato himself soon, in which case he won't need me anymore. Then what are they going to do with...*

"...my unique magic powers. Close your eyes."

The woman gives Darius a poke in the ribs, and he starts to play.

On the other side of the curtain, everything goes quiet. After about two minutes, he hears a groaning and a couple of swearwords. Then the patient—an emergency case who had come in with a broken arm—suddenly falls completely silent. Darius stops plucking and listens to the last notes fading away. There is a rustling sound.

"How...How did you...I don't understand it! The pain has gone! It's totally disappeared! You are...!" cries the patient.

Darius can see a figure leaping up behind the white curtain, as in a shadow play. The person is wildly waving an arm around.

"It's a *miracle*! You're a miracle worker, that's what you are! Incredible! I can move my arm quite normally now, look! Will you allow me to inform the media, Dr. Needham? I'm a journalist. I've never seen anything like it! No! Amazing! Absolutely amazing!"

Dr. Needham wriggles with modest embarrassment and waves his hand dismissively. "Oh, it was nothing. Not worth mentioning."

"Oh, but it is, Dr. Needham. It really is! It's worth far more of a mention than anything else we've had in our paper for years!" He takes a small camera out of his shirt pocket. "Let's have a smile, please!"

Then there are at least twenty flashes.

Dr. N's mother's face is radiant. "There you are. This is just the beginning," she whispers, patting Darius's cheek.

He turns his face away in disgust.

♪ ♪ ♪ ♪ ♪ ♪ ♪

A line has formed outside Ulrich Needham's practice. The day is warm and windy, and there are clouds of dust and cherry blossoms blowing across the sidewalk. A man lets out a barking cough, a mother is holding her screaming baby in her arms, and a woman in a wheelchair is leaning over a copy of the *Morning Post*. Also in the line are two slipped discs, one conjunctivitis, several hay fevers, four broken arms and/or legs, three influenzas, and one acute chicken pox. Cars are standing bumper to bumper, beeping impatiently, and the drivers are cursing one another because there's nowhere to park. From a distance more and more people are approaching, because they've all heard about Dr. Needham, the "wonder doctor." Since early morning, no one in the town has talked of anything else.

♪ ♪ ♪ ♪ ♪ ♪

On Wednesday morning, Mr. Archinola is sitting at a table in The Golden Crust. His beard is unkempt, and generally he doesn't look very happy at all. Lost in his thoughts, he has been stirring his coffee for at least three minutes.

"Have you seen the headlines in the *Morning Post*, Archie?" asks the owner of the bakery and puts the latest edition down in front of him, pointing to an article. "One more celebrity for The Golden Crust!"

Mr. Archinola reads:

Wonder Doctor Discovered

Dr. Ulrich Needham, young, fair-haired, and popular, has been in general practice in the St. Matthew's Church area for just three weeks, and in this short time, he has already displayed the most remarkable talents. All those who leave his office go home completely cured, no matter how serious or complicated their ailment may have been.

"I don't need to prescribe any medication," says Dr. Needham modestly. "The cure takes place as soon as the patient sits opposite me."

Broken bones mend and gashes close up in the healing presence of the wonder doctor. In his office, there is a unique atmosphere, which is enhanced by soft music.

"Yes, I love music," says the doctor. "Especially violin music."

His dedicated mother helps him in the practice in whatever way she can. "Even as a child he was different," Mrs. Needham recalls. "If he found a sick bird, he would touch it, and a moment later it would fly up into the sky completely cured," she says, still astonished by the child prodigy to whom she gave birth.

"Not worth mentioning," says the modest doctor, dismissively waving his hand. But the world around him will soon see things quite differently!

Mr. Archinola puts the paper on one side and at last slurps his lukewarm coffee. *I'd never have expected it from that pale-faced fellow,* he thinks to himself and for a moment is distracted from his melancholy. *So he's a wonder doctor! I must tell Alice about him. She should bring her mother to see him with her weak heart. Then she wouldn't have to keep going off to Italy. Because I miss her.* He lets out a loud cough, as if someone might have heard his thoughts and be ready to make fun of him. *And the boy—I miss him too.*

CHAPTER FOURTEEN

Indescribably Proud

Mrs. Needham is standing at the desk leafing nervously through the records of her son's patients.

"Try not to tear the index cards again, like you did the other day," says her son sarcastically. And when his mother fails to look up, he has another dig. "You still can't forget your old job, can you, Mother?"

"Oh, nonsense!" she barks. "Old job, old job! Our problems are totally different. And we've got them *now*! Today we had *one hundred and forty-four* patients, including two Frenchmen, four Spaniards, and three Poles."

She carries on leafing. "For next Monday we've got two Norwegians, one Italian, four Japanese, and an Icelander. Not to mention the massive lines outside the front door!" she shrills. There's no mistaking the fact that she's frightened. "News of your healing powers has spread like wildfire—even abroad now! The whole business has gone out of control. And there's not much I can do to help. I have to keep a permanent eye on the boy."

Ulrich is busy cutting out the newspaper article about the "wonder doctor," which he lovingly puts it in a glass-fronted frame. In the last few days, all the national newspapers have run stories about him. "Wonder Doctor Needham! The Hope of the Nation!" for example.

Or: "Inexplicable, but True: The Doctor Who Cures Every Illness." There is even one headline that reads: "Can This Man Walk on Water and Turn Stones into Bread?" Under each one is a large photo of him, looking serious and—in his eyes—extremely attractive.

With a blissful sigh, he now stands in front of a picture frame that looks smaller and older than the others, and on the glass of which is a thin layer of dust. A blurred photo bears an ornate caption that says, "Chamber of Horrors." Beneath it stand he and his mother, arm in arm and smiling into the camera.

"It's high time we got rid of the boy," he says, turning away from the photo and knocking another nail into the wall. Then he hangs the newly framed newspaper article on it. He leans his head to the side and looks admiringly at his work. "From next Monday, I shall start playing that thing myself. What that little runt does hardly needs an IQ of one-fifty! Or have you noticed any special complications in what he plays?"

"Actually, no," replies his mother after a moment's thought.

"Okay then. From Monday onwards, we'll simply deal with two patients at a time. You can take one, and I'll take the other. That'll double our speed. It's a good solution for the time being," he says, impressed with his own cleverness, and he takes off his glasses to clean them. "As soon as I'm world famous, we'll be able to afford just to treat two or three select patients a day." He grins and puts his glasses back on. "Or better still, just *one* a day. We shall earn such fabulous sums that we'll able to live a life of absolute luxury! The first thing we'll do is get ourselves a maid and...um...then a house. And at long last you can have a little night jacket made of chinchilla, eh, Mother? What do you say to that?"

Mrs. Needham smiles. "I am indescribably proud of you!"

Ulrich Needham's pale cheeks turn red. It's the first time that his mother has ever looked at him with admiration and has not called him "Bunny." He lets out a nasty snicker.

"Luckily there'll be no one expecting the boy next week. The violin-maker thinks he's in the children's home, and the children's home people think he's with the violin-maker. It's brilliant!" He roars with laughter.

"I just hope," says his mother, "that things won't go wrong without him."

Ulrich's expression darkens. "And what, may I ask, can go wrong?" he says, as if offended.

"I can't tell," his mother says softly. "But one never knows."

CHAPTER FIFTEEN

Fasten Your Belt and Back We Go

ey-Mey is trotting along on her way to school. She has spent half a week and the whole weekend doing math exercises, learning French vocab, and cleaning the house. Catastrophic! She has not played a single note! If she works it all out, the fact is that she hasn't played the violin now for twelve days. Her hands feel empty, and her head is in permanent darkness. She has a terrible longing to feel the violin on her shoulder and to lay the bow across the strings. But her parents insist that after school she goes straight home to study her math and French, because she's so awful at these subjects. Or she must scrub the hall, or do something magnificently "useful" like that, instead of wasting her time *fiddling, which won't get you anywhere.*

Mey-Mey looks up at the clear sky and the cherry trees, which with every gust of wind throw down their blossoms that sail like snowflakes onto the streets and into her hair. But these blossoms, which normally she loves so much, don't bring even a spark of light to Mey-Mey's heart today. Furiously she kicks a stone. *Why can't I do what I want to do?* she thinks. And what she wants to do is play the violin.

A sheet of newspaper flutters toward her feet, and another gust rustles it around her shins, as if the paper was trying to climb up her leg. Mey-Mey takes it off, straightens it out, and reads:

Wonder Doctor More
Famous by the Day!
"I heal the world!"

Beneath is a photo of a bespectacled man with little piggy eyes. She sits on a bench and goes on reading.

Wow! she thinks after a few moments. *This might be the answer! The wonder doctor could make my finger flexible again! Not for my sake—I really couldn't care less—but because of all those silly people who keep looking at me as if I consisted of a stiff finger and nothing else. Oh look, here comes Mey-Mey, the stiff finger! How's the poor creature ever going to play the violin properly with that? Oh, what a shame!*

Mey-Mey pulls a face and starts thinking about the wonder doctor again. *Then maybe I'd finally get the chance to show what I can do! Yes, maybe…*

She suddenly hears the church clock striking.

"Oh shoot, now I'm going to be late, and it's math too!" she says aloud and then rolls up the newspaper and throws it in the trash can.

♪ ♪ ♪   ♪   ♪ ♪♪

After the fourth lesson, Mey-Mey can't stand it anymore. She skips the double period of French, hops unseen over the playground wall, and, with a determined look on her face, hurries off in a totally different direction from usual.

Although she's gained time by playing truant, she still needs to hurry, because her parents will be furious with her if she doesn't get home punctually after she's seen the doctor. Mey-Mey runs. Only when she sees the crowd of people outside the dazzling white villa on Angel Street does she slow down and then finally stop some distance away.

A van bearing the logo of a well-known TV company is parked outside the villa, and there's a cameraman with a TV camera perched on his shoulder. The people in the line are being interviewed. One after another they're subjected to having a thick red microphone shoved in front of their mouths.

Mey-Mey doesn't have time to stand in this endless line of people! Slowly she approaches them. The air is full of white birch pollen that floats around them like tiny angels. When she walks past the line, getting ever closer to the entrance to the villa, on which stands the brand new brass sign that says in black letters, Dr. Needham, General Practitioner, she can already hear the first outraged cries.

"Hey, go to the back!"

"What d'you think you're doing? Let me out!"

"I've been waiting five hours, girl, so you can wait your turn!"

On the steps leading to the front door, Mey-Mey suddenly rolls her eyes and then collapses to the ground like a rag doll.

♪ ♪ ♪ ♪ ♪ ♪

"The next two patients, please." Ulrich releases the button on his intercom and grins at his mother. "It should all go like clockwork today, don't you think?"

"We make a marvelous team," gushes his mother and gives a little cough as·the door opens.

"Do sit down," Ulrich tells the young man with large bandages all over his chin and cheek. "And just put the money in there." He points to a bucket with a slit in the lid, on which is written: Fee for Miracles.

"And would you please come over here to me?" warbles his mother, beckoning to an elderly lady to come and sit opposite her at the desk. The woman drags one leg, leans her crutch against the side of the desk, and sits down. She painstakingly fishes a large bundle of cash out of her purse, leans over, and with eyes full of hope sticks the money in the bucket.

"It's because of my polio," she begins, but Mrs. Needham puts her finger to her lips, like a mother telling a noisy child to be quiet in church.

"There's no need to explain," she says quietly. "Just close your eyes."

"And you too," says Ulrich, bestowing an artificial smile on the young man, who is squirming uncomfortably on his chair.

Tensely, the two patients close their eyes and wait. There is a deathly silence in the room.

"Fasten your belts, and back we go!" shouts Ulrich suddenly.

The two of them open their eyes wide. His mother gives him a horrified look. He himself is shocked and claps a hand to his mouth.

"Just my little joke," he says hastily and coughs into his fist. "Forgive me. And just close your eyes again. Good, that's it."

When both of them have closed their eyes again, Mrs. Needham, with a furious grimace, taps her forehead as if to ask, *Have you gone crazy?* He takes no notice, but places Pizzicato on his lap, as he has seen Darius do, and begins to pluck the strings. He puts an extremely self-important expression on his face, even though his patients can't see it. Ulrich Needham is nothing if not an actor. *If you're going to play the role,* he says to himself, *then play it properly.* He raises his eyebrows and flares his nostrils, because that's how he imagines a true musician would look when he played.

The sounds that he produces from the violin are nothing like those that Darius makes, but are harsher and more abrupt—he can hear that for himself—but he figures that won't matter.

"Okay," he says at last, then stops plucking and plunks Pizzicato down against his desk. "And now, ladies and gentlemen, let's have those little eyes open again, shall we? The...uh...performance is over! So now let's have a look, eh?" He stands up and tears the bandage off the young man's cheek.

"Ouch!" screams the man and puts his hand up to his cheek.

"Let me see!" snaps Ulrich and pushes the young man's hand to one side. "Hm," he says then and pushes his slipping spectacles back onto the bridge of his nose. "Hm. Well, yes, that does look a lot, lot better! And by the time you get home, it will be completely healed. Take my word for it." Hastily he sticks the bandage back on.

"What about you?" he asks, grabbing the elderly woman under the armpits and roughly pulling her out of her chair. "Now just take a few steps, madam. Come on, come on. Don't pretend you're too tired!" He lets go of her and gives her a little shove.

She takes a wobbly step forward, staggers on the spot, and collapses with a dull thud onto the linoleum-covered floor.

"Oh my God, Bunny...um...I mean, oh my God!" cries Mrs. Needham, aghast, and she helps the groaning patient back on her feet, then quickly thrusts the crutch under her arm.

"Yes, well," says Ulrich in a firm voice, "as I said, the cure will be completed very rapidly before you even get home. Now, if you'd be so kind, there are about a hundred and fifty more patients waiting outside to see my mother and me, so have a nice day!"

Impatiently he ushers the bewildered woman and the baffled man out of the office and slams the door behind them.

"What does it mean, Mother?" he moans. "Why didn't it work?"

He stamps his foot. His mother puts her arm around his waist.

"But Bunny, darling! No virtuoso ever fell from heaven! First you've got to get used to playing the violin. You'll soon get the hang of it." She pinches his cheek. "After all, that gash already looked a lot better. And the woman did take one step without her crutch! Isn't that a success? And if it comes to the worst, we've still got the boy!" she says, pointing downwards.

♪ ♪ ♪ ♪ ♪ ♪ ♪

"Hey!" cries Darius and kicks the wall of the cellar in which he's been locked for the last two days and nights. He knows that no one can hear him, no matter how loud he shouts or how hard he hammers the massive metal door, which is so thickly and softly padded inside that any blow will be swallowed up as if by a cushion of feathers. Not even the slightest sound can escape.

Angrily he kicks the padded door again and then throws himself down on the mattress on the damp gray-green concrete of the floor.

He hasn't touched the bottle of water and the bar of chocolate that Mrs. Needham, with her twisted smile, put out for him sometime this morning. His head is swirling. *How can I get out of here?* This must be the hundredth time he's asked himself that question and looked around for a way out.

There's no window in the cellar. It's dimly lit by a light-bulb hanging from the ceiling, which curves up into a kind of vault at the top. Close to Darius's mattress is a crumpled, dried-up spider in a torn web. Black plastic pipes with white splotches of paint run like snakes along the masonry walls. Darius breathes in the sickly dampness of the air. Piled up in one of the arches are a wooden sled, an old paint bucket with a solidified brush, and a vacuum cleaner. A toilet and a washbasin are behind a plywood door. Beside the main door hangs a fire extinguisher. He has scanned these things so often with his eyes that he could draw them blindfolded. This place is ten times worse than the garden shed. Not even Queenie can get him out of here.

CHAPTER SIXTEEN
The Lovely Old Jacket

"**S**o, you fainted?" says Mrs. Needham, looking dubiously at her son. "Could it be that you simply wanted to cut in line?" she asks and brusquely motions to Mey-Mey to sit down on the chair in front of the chrome-and-glass desk.

Mey-Mey obeys. *They're not exactly friendly people*, she thinks to herself. *But the main thing is that they'll see me now, and then I can go straight home.* She looks around, taking it all in.

Every inch of the mint-green painted walls is covered with newspaper cuttings, proclaiming the "wonder doctor." Climbing up around the window frame is some shining plastic ivy. On the desk are a travel brochure and a fur coat catalog, which Ulrich Needham hurriedly stuffs into a drawer when he realizes that Mey-Mey is looking at it. On the other side of the room is a white curtain that has been partially opened. Behind it is a mat, and on the mat, carelessly discarded, lies—

Ulrich bangs his fist on the top of his desk. "Okay," he says in harsh tone, "let me tell you that we have no time for little actresses here."

At the moment when she is about to raise her stiff finger and speak, Mey-Mey's eyes again fall on the mat behind the curtain. She pauses in confusion. What's lying there—no doubt about it—is Darius's lovely old jacket! *So could it be that he's here as well?* Not knowing what to do, she stands up. *Maybe he's in the waiting room!*

Her thoughts are rudely interrupted.

Mrs. Needham has seen the girl's face as she spotted the boy's jacket, which stupidly, has not yet been cleared away. And she's noticed something else too: the brown spot on Mey-Mey's neck, which is only to be seen on violin and viola players who play regularly.

Coldly she says to her son, "This girl is not ill. But she knows more than is good for you and me, you can bet your life on it." With a pad of cotton in her hand, she goes up to Mey-Mey—who is taken completely by surprise—and presses it over her face. "Now you can really faint away, you little beast!" she whispers.

In no time, Mey-Mey's senses are deadened, and she falls into a deep sleep.

"Quick, let's get her into the cellar!" whispers Ulrich.

Two minutes later, the patients in the waiting room are surprised to see that, in spite of all their huge workload of healing, the wonder doctor and his mother still have time to hurry past them, smiling sweetly and carrying a giant cardboard box for a television set.

♪ ♪ ♪ ♪ ♪ ♪

Five minutes later, Darius is surprised when the partners in crime fling open the padded door and dump a large cardboard box on the floor. When the door slams shut again, once again the cellar is left to its musty silence.

Except that there is now a soft breathing sound, and it's not coming from him.

"Mey-Mey!"

Darius looks into the box with amazement and opens it with a rip. Gently he lifts his friend out, carries her to the mattress, and carefully lays her down.

"Can you hear me?"

Shyly he touches her cheeks. But her eyes remain closed. Darius picks up the bottle of water and holds it to her lips. The water runs down her chin. He quickly wipes it dry with the sleeve of his sweater.

They've drugged Mey-Mey too, he thinks. *But why? What has she got to do with all this?* He lays her head in his lap and sits motionless looking at her. *This is not where I'd hoped to see you again,* he says to himself. *We'd both have been a lot happier at the musical evening with Schubert.* Softly he strokes her smooth black hair.

Then suddenly Mey-Mey's eyes open, and she's looking straight at him.

"Darius!" she murmurs. "Where are we? What are you doing here?"

Darius is really happy that Mey-Mey is able to talk now. "We're in a cellar," he answers. "Unfortunately."

Once again he supports her head and holds the bottle to her lips. This time she drinks.

"Thank you." She lays her head back in his lap. With a sigh she closes her eyes again. "We'll find a way out," she says, and her voice is firm and clear despite her drowsiness.

Darius tenderly strokes her hair again and then her cheeks. "Yes, we'll find a way out," he says. "Definitely."

CHAPTER SEVENTEEN

Queenie Wakes Up

🎵

"**Y**ou're making a viola da gamba, Mr. Archinola? Oh, that's exquisite!" Alice's mother is standing in Mr. Archinola's workshop and admiringly clasps her hands in front of her mouth. She bends, as if in prayer, over the wooden interior of the viola, to which the carved neck with its elegant scroll and ribs has already been attached. "All my life I've loved gamba music," she enthuses. "That dark, elegiac twilight tone—it's so solemn and always sounds as if it's harboring some strange secret."

Alice is surprised that her eighty-two-year-old mother is able to discuss the qualities of a viola da gamba with a master violin-maker. And that she can do so after they'd touched down only a few hours ago! Archie had called her, sounding very excited, and had begged her to come back as quickly as possible with her mother. He'd told her some garbled story about a wonder doctor. And that he'd missed her. And that the boy had left. So Alice had booked the next available flight, and now she was here with her mother.

"Shouldn't we be thinking about our appointment with this wonder doctor?" she asks, stepping between her mother and her friend.

Absentmindedly Mr. Archinola glances at his watch. "We should indeed!" he exclaims. "We're already late!"

And the three of them hurry out of the house.

Soon afterward, they're sitting in the overcrowded waiting room of the villa on Angel Street. The telephone at the reception desk never stops ringing.

"Dr. Needham's office, Angelica speaking, how can I help you?" warbles the receptionist like a singing doll.

If the patients were a little more observant, they would realize that her voice has gotten quieter during the last few calls, and finally she has turned her back on them and lowered her head.

"*What?*" she whispers, clearly dumbfounded. "You've got what? All of a sudden your leg is paralyzed, though Dr. Needham treated you for hives? Uh-huh. Yes, I'll tell him."

Trembling, she puts the receiver down, but before she can go in and inform her employer about his patient's new problem, the phone rings again.

"Your husband has a temperature of a hundred and five degrees and a rash all over his body after coming to us with a paralyzed leg—yes, I understand, I've got it." She is close to tears. "At least has his paralyzed leg been cured?" she ventures to ask, her voice now hoarse. "Oh, it hasn't. Now both legs are paralyzed. Of course I can understand that you're upset. I can understand completely. I'll inform the doctor as soon as I have a second...Hello? Hellooo?"

The caller has hung up.

Angelica, the receptionist, sinks back on her chair. *Is something wrong with the doctor?* she wonders anxiously. All day long it's been one disaster after another! Everybody seems to have been worse off after the treatment than before! No, not just "seems"—they really have! When the telephone rings again, she picks it up and immediately puts it down again. Then she stares in embarrassment out into empty space.

The waiting room door swings open.

"I want to sit at the front!" pipes the squeaky voice of a little girl.

And a man's deep voice answers, "But someone's already sitting there, as you can see. So please just stay with me."

Mr. Archinola turns around. Then he gets up and bows to the astonished carer. "Good afternoon," he says courteously. And he shakes Queenie's tiny hand. "We've met before, haven't we?"

Queenie nods. "Have you still got my daffodils?" she asks.

"I'm afraid they faded away," says Mr. Archinola, in a tone of deep regret.

Ben perches on a window ledge, as there are no vacant chairs in the waiting room. Queenie takes her much-too-large pink backpack off her back and leans against the long legs of the giant, who puts his hands on her shoulders.

"What a nice coincidence, seeing you here, Mr. Archinola," says Ben, smiling. "I've come here because of our Queenie—she hasn't grown an inch for three years," he explains, stroking Queenie's hair. "This doctor's supposed to possess magic powers. But what I'd really like to know is, how's our Darius getting on with you? Is he giving you a lot of trouble?"

The friendly expression on Mr. Archinola's face suddenly freezes over. At the same time, he raises his eyebrows and his ears. He opens his mouth, closes it, opens it, gasps for air, and then shuts it again.

Queenie gives him a curious look. "What's the matter with the violin man?" she asks, tugging at Ben's fingers till the knuckles crack. "He looks like a fish."

Ben also wants to know. "Is something wrong?"

Mr. Archinola tries to pull himself together. "The boy... isn't he..." he stammers, and gesticulates wildly with his hands, "...isn't he with you in the children's home?"

Ben looks at him in alarm. "No. Darius is supposed to be with you!" Then after a moment's silence, he says softly, "Oh my God!"

"You're all looking as if you've just seen Beelzebub!" laughs Alice's mother, coming over to join them. But when she sees Mr. Archinola's stony face, she turns deadly serious. A few of the bored patients prick up their ears.

"Let's go outside," whispers Ben. "I think there are more important things than a visit to the wonder doctor!"

♪ ♪ ♪ ♪ ♪ ♪ ♪

Scarcely have they gone outside when they hear the trembling voice of the receptionist. "We're closing for today!" she calls out. "The doctor and his esteemed mother are exhausted, and they're urgently in need of a break from their miracles. We ask you for your understanding, and please come back tomorrow."

A flood of furious patients comes out of the front door, while the people in the line start protesting.

"So you got this phone call on Friday and haven't heard anything from Darry since then?" Ben asks Mr. Archinola.

The four of them are standing in a circle near the steps leading to the villa.

"That's right," says Mr. Archinola, still sounding horrified. "I spoke to him in person! Otherwise, I wouldn't have believed any of it."

Alice wraps her knitted jacket more tightly around her and puts her hand on his arm. "I think we should go to the police right away instead of wasting more time."

"You're right," says the disconsolate Mr. Archinola. "I just hope Darius is all right," he adds in a quiet voice. "I feel so guilty now!"

"Have you seen Queenie anywhere?" Ben is turning to look in all directions.

"I think she popped back into the doctor's a few minutes ago," says Alice's mother.

"Just wait, and I'll go and get her," says Ben and disappears into the villa.

Scarcely two minutes have gone by when the front door opens again, and he comes out, leading Queenie by the hand. With her large pink backpack, she looks as if she's just come back from hiking.

"Just imagine, she was exploring the examination room!" says Ben. "Fortunately, there was no one in there."

He ruffles Queenie's hair, and she grins.

"And now let's get to the nearest police station as fast as we can. We'll take my car."

During the drive, they discuss every detail of the case and decide that once they've talked to the police, they'll also search for Darius themselves.

"It could be a long night," remarks Ben.

Alice's mother is snoring softly in the backseat, with her mouth open. Next to her sits Queenie. She has both her arms around her backpack, as if it is a teddy bear.

Alice looks anxiously out of the window. *I only hope nothing has happened to the boy,* she thinks.

♪ ♪ ♪ ♪ ♪ ♪

For hours Queenie had helped in the search for Darius. But with no success. Now she's tossing and turning in bed. She mumbles softly, as if she were talking to someone.

When she wakes up, the day is dawning. Suddenly she remembers something very important. Something she noticed yesterday in the office of that weird wonder doctor, but then forgot again.

She slides out of bed quietly, so as not to disturb Jessica, and scurries down the cold staircase to the carer's bedroom. It's Ben who is on night duty. Without knocking, she slips through the door and creeps up to the narrow wooden bed.

Ben's long hair is spread out over the pillow like fine, wavy lines in the sand. Queenie thinks he looks like a sleeping angel—or maybe a dead angel. Anyway, he looks rather handsome.

"Hey!" she whispers and shakes his angelic shoulders. "Heeey!" she then shouts, because although he grunts, he doesn't seem to want to wake up.

"Eh…what? What's the matter?" Ben sits up as straight as a candle.

Queenie switches on the bedside lamp, and Ben blinks.

"I know where Darry is," she says cheerfully. "I saw his totally favorite old jacket."

Ben grabs hold of her hand. Now he, too, is wide awake. "Where?" he asks.

Queenie holds a hand over his ear and whispers something.

"I'll just get my clothes on," he cries, "and off we'll go. And we'll tell Mr. Archinola right away!"

CHAPTER EIGHTEEN
Ready to Fire
♫

Mey-Mey puts a piece of chocolate in her mouth. "Ugh, ugh, I shall never eat Snickers again once we're out of here," she groans and stands up. "Eventually someone's bound to come looking for us." She drums her fingers impatiently on the fire extinguisher next to the door.

Suddenly Darius's eyes narrow to slits. Then he slaps his forehead with the palm of his hand. "Hey, I've got an idea!"

With a single bound, he leaps up from the mattress. Then he lets out a grunt as he jerks the fire extinguisher away from the wall and deposits it on the concrete floor with a metallic thump. "The thing's been staring us in the face for hours, and we never realized it!"

"What thing? What are you talking about?" asks Mey-Mey, looking puzzled.

"We could give them a nasty shock with this," says Darius, grinning at Mey-Mey.

He has told her the whole story of Pizzicato, and so now she knows everything.

"You mean we should shoot them? With the fire extinguisher?"

"Exactly!"

Her face lights up. "Not bad!"

She bends down and, with a nimble movement of her fingers, removes the safety catch on the fire extinguisher. As always, her left forefinger sticks out stiffly from the rest, but that doesn't seem to bother her.

"Take it," she says and holds the hose out to Darius. "Don't be scared." She quickly presses and releases a lever, and there is a loud hiss. "Now it's ready to fire." She fetches the sled from the corner, puts it next to the fire extinguisher, and sits down. Then she taps the wooden slats next to her. "Coming?"

Darius joins her. "Where did you learn how to do that?" he asks.

"You mean how to eat chocolate?" replies Mey-Mey, wiping her lips.

"How to use a fire extinguisher," he replies seriously.

"Can't remember," Mey-Mey answers slowly and with a frown. "I try lots of things. I'll tackle whatever's there to be tackled. So I can soon cope with any problems and I don't have to keep asking people for help. Then there's more time to do really important things."

"Like music," says Darius and gives her an admiring sideways look.

"Exactly," she says. "Shall I show you how to use the fire extinguisher?"

Darius laughs. "I can do it pretty well myself, thanks."

"Great! You might say that we're—"

"The perfect team!" says Darius with a nod. Then he says softly, "Listen. I'll help you with your finger as soon as I've got Pizzicato back, okay? It'll do that."

After a moment's silence, Mey-Mey replies a little hesitantly, "That's really nice of you. I was thinking about that too. It would be really good, because…it would be wonderful for my parents…and good for Mr. Archinola and for—" She breaks off.

"The musical world?" asks Darius.

"Yes," says Mey-Mey. "They all keep going on about my finger, as if the rest of me didn't count."

Suddenly she grasps his arm.

"Shhh! I heard something," she whispers and jumps up. "Are you ready to fire?"

Darius also leaps to his feet. "Aye, aye," he acknowledges quietly and balances the fire extinguisher on his arm.

Mey-Mey grabs hold of the hose and aims it at the padded door. A moment later, the door opens.

"Fire!" they both shout at the same time.

♪ ♪ ♪ ♪ ♪ ♪

Two seconds later, there's an almighty hullabaloo. A solid stream of white powder hits the two flabbergasted people in the doorway full in the face. One of them collapses to the floor with shock, pulling the other down as well. Somebody screams, and everything is hissing and stinking like crazy.

"Let's get out!" cries Darius before he drops the fire extinguisher onto the concrete with a loud crash, grabs Mey-Mey by the hand, and leaps with her over the foaming white bodies on the cellar floor. They race up the stairs and push open the door to the examination room.

"I'll get Pizzicato!" yells Darius.

He quickly looks around the room. Mey-Mey is right behind him.

"Have you got it?" she asks, panting for air.

Darius pulls the white curtain aside, and when he fails to find the violin, he rushes across to the desk. He searches under it, on it, and behind it, and then he tears open the doors to all the cupboards in the office. Nothing.

"I can't find it!" he says. "There's something really fishy going on here. Everything seems so deserted."

Then the two of them get a real shock.

"Darius!" somebody shouts.

"Mey-Mey!" splutters another.

"Darry!" squeaks another.

They both turn around. Apart from three open mouths, they can hardly recognize anything in the three figures now standing in the room covered from head to toe with white-gray powder.

"Mr....Archi...Archinola!" gasps Mey-Mey incredulously.

"Ben?" asks Darius. "Queenie?"

Darius and Mey-Mey look at each other in bewilderment.

"Oh God, it wasn't the Needhams! They've escaped!" cries a thunderstruck Mey-Mey.

"And they've taken Pizzicato with them!" says Darius.

CHAPTER NINETEEN
Missing
♪

I n the evening, Mr. Archinola is putting a thick chunk of wood on the blazing fire in the fireplace. Glittering sparks leap up into the air, and there's a loud crunching and crackling. Alice gently pulls a cover over the sleeping Darius and then leans back against the felt-covered sofa.

"I think he's got a fever," she says quietly.

"Yes, he gets it when he's worked up about something," whispers Mr. Archinola, putting a couple of potatoes wrapped in tinfoil on the fire. "It generally only lasts one night," he adds, with the knowing air of a specialist.

That same morning the violin-maker and the carer from the children's home had been to the police to call off the search. They'd also telephoned Mey-Mey's parents, because they, too, had reported their daughter missing and were in a terrible state. With a mixture of a big reprimand and an even bigger hug, they had fetched their darling daughter that afternoon from Mr. Archinola's. Ben had gone back to the children's home with Queenie. Darius was supposed to follow the next day when he'd had enough rest. The grown-ups all agreed—the project had to end. All this excitement was too much for a boy like Darius. He should return to his "familiar surroundings," so that he could "relax," and just come back for the last time to Mr. Archinola's on Sunday for the musical soirée.

The reason why Dr. Needham and his mother had kidnapped Darius in the first place seemed pretty obvious to the grown-ups: these two villains would soon have demanded ransom money for him, because they thought Darius must be a relative of the prosperous violin-maker! And Mey-Mey had seen through their villainy and so had also fallen into their clutches! It all added up, and Darius and Mey-Mey had exchanged secret looks and maintained a grave-like silence. Not a word did they speak about Pizzicato.

In place of the missing persons announcement came a "wanted" notice for the Needhams—for fraud and kidnapping. The police had been inundated with complaints from furious patients, and the hunt had been given high priority. There were even reports on TV about the "wonder doctor and his mother on the run," and their photos were plastered all over the bus stops and billboards in the town.

"But why did you make me come back from Italy if you thought these Needhams were swindlers?" asks Alice, stretching out on the thick, comfortable carpet.

"Ah, well...I...um..." Mr. Archinola strokes his beard, which he has not brushed even once today thanks to all the comings and goings, and stuck to which there are still some flecks of fire extinguisher powder. "I...um...I just thought..." He searches for an explanation. Then with a sigh he gives up. "I...um..."—he frantically wiggles a poker between the burning pieces of wood—"...well...missed you so much, you see."

"I missed you too, Archie," Alice says very simply.

Mr. Archinola spikes one of the baked potatoes and takes it out of the fire. "We can eat now," he says with a laugh, partly because the potato smells great and partly because he's overjoyed at what Alice has just said.

"Archie?" Alice holds out her plate.

"Yes?" Mr. Archinola puts the potato on it.

"How about the two of us going together to Cremona sometime soon?"

"Alice?" Mr. Archinola asks in return. *When, if not now?* he asks himself. Here and now, in this warm glow with the appetizing smell of the potatoes, he summons up all his courage.

"Yes?" asks Alice.

"How about the two of us…maybe…getting married there?"

The room goes very quiet. There is nothing but the crackling of the fire and the smell of the baked potatoes.

And although Darius has a fever and his eyes are closed, he is actually awake and has two perfectly functioning ears. And when, in the warm, dry stillness of his guest room, he hears Alice's answer, a smile spreads all the way across his face. And then at last he falls into a deep sleep.

CHAPTER TWENTY

It Doesn't Belong to Us

♫

"**W**oo-hoo! Slugboy's messed everything up as usual!"

It's early Wednesday afternoon, and Max is smirking as Darius puts a duffel bag down in their room. Max and his friend Daniel have draped themselves over the chairs at the writing table, as if they were both made of rubber.

"What are you doing here?" asks Darius as he takes off his "lovely old" jacket. "Is it lunchtime at Auto Frederick?"

Max has been scratching the top of the table with a nail file, and now he flings it across the room. It clinks as it hits the wall and falls to the floor.

"You stupid slug, what you gibberin' about? Can't you keep yer silly trap shut *just for once*? Auto Frederick is super uncool! So I scrammed!" He raises a corner of his mouth and sneers, "What about you? Too stupid fer the violin twit or what?" He lets out an exaggerated laugh. "Bound to've been, with your IQ of under fifty!"

He pokes Daniel in the ribs, and Daniel laughs as if Max had just pressed the "silly laugh" button.

Nothing's changed, thinks Darius disconsolately, and pulls open the zipper of his duffel bag. The pink radio shines out from on top, like the memory of an earlier life that, from now on, he will have to resume. In silence he takes it out and puts it beside his bed.

"Let's vamoose," says Max and then gives Darius a clout on the head as he goes past and tugs Daniel out of the room by his hood. "Otherwise, he'll drive me up the wall."

Scarcely has Darius finished unpacking and pressing the flat, cool side of his new chisel—a farewell present from Mr. Archinola—against the painful spot that Max had clouted, when Queenie wanders into the room. She's dressed from head to toe in pink, because for some time now pink has been her favorite color.

"Darry!" She takes a run and comes leaping into his arms.

He holds her tight.

"Will you be staying with us again forever now?" she asks, pressing her cheek against his.

"Looks like it," murmurs Darius and gently puts Queenie down on the floor. "Look, I've got something for you." He picks up the pink radio and holds it out to her. "Goes with your outfit."

Queenie grabs the radio, without a second look, and immediately clasps it under her arm. It looks as if it's always been there.

"Why don't you want it anymore?" she asks, but there's no way she's going to give it back again. A present is a present!

"No particular reason," says Darius. If he doesn't hear any more music, he hopes that maybe he won't miss Mr. Archinola and the workshop quite so much.

"I want to show you something, so you must come to my room," commands Queenie.

Darius wants to shake his head in refusal, because he's feeling tired and grumpy—Ben calls that "having the grumps"—and in fact he'd rather be on his own, but then she adds, with a conspiratorial air, "It's got something to do with music."

This arouses his curiosity. "Okay, but only for a moment, okay?" he says and lets Queenie tow him along by his sweater sleeve out of the room and across the hall.

Queenie keeps a tight hold of his sleeve and pushes the door to her room with her shoulder. Darius is quite dazzled by all the pink: pink walls, pink curtains, pink bedsheets, shiny pink stickers on the bedside table, and a giant pink teddy bear. Apparently it doesn't seem to bother her roommate, Jessica.

He whistles through his teeth. "We'll soon have to change your name," he says, "from Queenie to Rosie!"

Queenie takes no notice. She flits across to the bunk bed, and her pigtail wiggles from side to side behind her like a windshield wiper. First she looks quickly under the bed, and then she looks at Darius. But she doesn't do anything.

"What's wrong?" he asks and sits down on the nearest chair. "Are you going to do a dance for me, or what?"

Queenie gives him a strange look.

"Okay, go on, dance," Darius orders and folds his hands behind his head. "I'm the jury, right?"

Then Queenie flings herself onto the bed and begins to howl. "Owowowowowow!"

"Oh Lord, what's wrong? What's the matter with you?" Darius is shocked and jumps up, then kneels in front of her. "Hey, come on. Say something, Queenie!"

With a snivel, she whines, "Don't tell on me, Darry! I brought it with me!"

"It?" asks Darius uncomprehendingly. "What's 'it'?"

Queenie's face crumples up again, in readiness for the tears. "The viiiolin!" she whimpers.

Darius gapes. "You've got a *violin*? Where on earth did *you* get a violin from, Queenie?" he asks in disbelief.

"From…from…" Queenie is shaking with all her sobs. "I took it from the wonder doctor's place, where your jacket was hanging. It was so pretty. So I stuck it in my backpack. But you mustn't tell anyone, not even Ben!"

Then again she starts howling like a wolf cub. Darius takes her little hand in his. "Shh, Queenie, shh, it'll be all right. Don't worry." He pulls a handkerchief out of his pants pocket and holds it up to her running nose. "Blow," he says very gently. Then he wipes away her tears and asks, "Has the violin done anything special since it's been with you?"

Queenie nods. "It glowed once. Like a sort of blue."

"Have you played it?" he asks, because he knows that Pizzicato has to be handled very carefully, and so he needs to be quite sure.

Queenie shakes her head. "Jessie would have noticed," she says softly.

Darius breathes a sigh of relief and strokes Queenie's hair. "The violin's name is Pizzicato, by the way. And it doesn't belong to us."

"But it didn't belong to the wonder doctor either, did it?" says Queenie.

"No, least of all to him!" answers Darius.

As he did a long time ago in the violin-maker's guest room, he now sits cross-legged on the floor and pulls the violin from under Queenie's bed. It lets out a mellow sound.

"Hey, Pizzicato," he whispers. "Pizzicato, magic violin! It's lucky I've got you back!"

Gently he strokes its strings.

You're really beautiful, he thinks. *But I've lost interest in your miracles now. So I'm going to take you home.*

CHAPTER TWENTY-ONE

The Second Violin

🎵

"**A**re Mey-Mey's parents here?" whispers Mr. Archinola nervously. It's the following Sunday, and he has a quick look into the salesroom. About thirty people are sitting there. The men are wearing suits, and their black shoes are shining. The women are dressed in all their finery and have put their hair up. On a wooden platform is a little semicircle of music stands, a cello on its endpin, and four empty chairs. All eyes are on it, and the air is full of expectant whisperings and murmurings.

"They're sitting in the back row. Look, over there," Alice answers quietly, pointing to a woman and a man. Next to them sits Mey-Mey, who is chatting away animatedly. And next to her, with eyes shining, Darius has just taken his seat, and beside him is Queenie, who is swinging her legs backward and forward because she's never been to a concert before and is very excited. Just for today she's put a pink bow in her hair, and it's bigger than her head. She thinks she looks like a butterfly, or perhaps an Easter bunny—she likes them both. Alice gives the violin-maker a kiss on the cheek, and he blushes with pleasure.

"Are all the musicians here?" she asks.

"All except for the second violin," he replies, looking at his watch. "No idea where she can be."

After about ten minutes, Mr. Kaplan steps onto the wooden platform with his viola and his newly strung bow, followed by a redheaded lady in a blue silk dress, who sits down behind her cello. Next comes a man in a suit, carrying a violin. They all bow.

"Where on earth is the second violin?" asks Mr. Archinola, now beginning to get really worried.

The telephone rings.

"Violin-Maker's Archinola."

Mr. Archinola listens without saying a word. He slowly turns pale. "Right," he says in the end, "in that case there's nothing we can do. So whether we like it or not, the concert"—he glances at Alice—"will have to be canceled." In despair he adds, "But I've got a room full of people! I'm sorry, I'll have to hang up."

"Oh dear!" moans Alice, appalled. "What's happened?"

"She says she's ill, but it sounds to me like stage fright. This was her first concert."

Without another word, Mr. Archinola squeezes her arm and then strides into the salesroom, walking past all the guests, who are looking at him expectantly. His shoe heels click through the room like audio exclamation marks. Then he steps onto the platform.

"Ladies and gentlemen, I'm sorry to have to tell you that the second violin has just rung to say she's been taken ill." A murmur of consternation buzzes through the room. Mr. Archinola clenches his hands together. "It's extremely embarrassing for me, knowing that you've made the effort to come here all for nothing. Of course, you're invited to stay and have a glass of wine with me and my fiancée." He puts his fingertips together. "I really am terribly sorry, but there's nothing I can do. That's all I can say."

The violin-maker has already stepped down from the platform when a little voice pipes up. "Mey-Mey can play the violin! You can, can't you, Mey-Mey?"

The guests turn around and look at the little girl with the giant bow in her hair.

All this time, Darius has not been able to think of anything else but Pizzicato, which is in his duffel bag under the chair. For the thousandth time he's imagining telling Mr. Archinola why he took the violin out of its cabinet and thus started the whole wretched affair. But now, as he looks at Mey-Mey, these thoughts suddenly stop racing around his head. He says, "Yes, you should play. You've practiced Schubert so many times!"

Mey-Mey's parents give him a look that could kill.

"Well," says Mr. Archinola hesitantly, "what do you think, Mey-Mey? Are you prepared to take a shot at the second violin?"

The audience has been holding its breath, but now a few people call out.

"Go on, girl, play for us."

"It'll be a farce! You can't play Schubert as if it was 'Ring Around the Rosie'!"

"Let the girl play!"

"I'm leaving if you're going to have kids playing."

"Isn't that the handicapped girl?"

Darius takes Pizzicato out of his duffel bag and then presses Mey-Mey's hand. "Go on, you can do it!" he whispers, and in his two hands he holds the beautiful violin out towards her. "Take it. The violin will help you."

Mey-Mey looks across at the stage and then at Darius. "No, Darry," she says, putting one hand on Pizzicato's strings and the other on his shoulder. "I'll try my own magic up there."

She stands up.

She goes past the rows of chairs, past the line of cellos on the walls, and past all the eyes that are looking at her. She goes to the case near the display cabinet. She bends and opens the clasps. Gently she lifts out the violin on which she has practiced so often over the last few months. She picks up the bow and climbs onto the platform, which greets her with a soft creak. She gives a slight bow to the audience, which has now fallen as quiet as a churchyard. Then she sits on the front chair, her back ruler-straight. She nods solemnly to the other musicians, places her chin against the chinrest, and lays the violin on her shoulder.

"Isn't that great!" whispers Alice, who has sat next to Mr. Archinola and Darius. Queenie has clambered onto Alice's lap and is now leaning back against her breast.

"Let's wait and see," says Mr. Archinola, who is still trembling from the shock, and he dabs the sweat from his brow with his handkerchief. "It's not going to be easy for her."

At this moment, the music begins.

With bated breath Darius watches every movement that Mey-Mey makes, and he hears every note that soars from her violin. To him it sounds as if someone has opened a floodgate in a river, and the dammed-up water is now flowing forth with a soft and beautiful, but powerful rhythm.

He also looks at the other musicians. The violin appears tiny on the arm of the big man in the dark suit. His pant legs are at half-mast, and his shoes are as brightly polished as crystals of ice. At this moment he raises his eyebrows, and the tone of the violin becomes gentler. The notes hover delicately between the guests. And then the music becomes wilder! Mr. Kaplan saws fiercely at his viola, and his gray hair flies up into the air like wings and then flops down again.

Minute by minute, the music floods deeper and deeper into Darius's body. The notes, which fit together so beautifully, bring order to everything that had been lying higgledy-piggledy inside him.

And Mey-Mey! She plays as if the violin was actually part of her neck and shoulder. Her cheek nestles so snugly against it, and the two seem so closely bound together, that Darius feels almost jealous! All four musicians turn the pages of their scores at the same time and quickly fix the paper with the ends of their bows before they play on. Their breathing provides a gentle, regular accompaniment to the music. The sun is low now and sheds a deep glow over the room. Slowly the light creeps over the face of the first violin and onto the white paper of the score. Then suddenly it covers Mey-Mey's face in a radiant glow, like a golden fleece. She seems to be unaware of everything around her. Again and again she whips the bow vigorously away from her violin, as if she has to hold herself back from playing on when it's no longer her turn to do so. The breath of all four eases in and out. Scrolls and hands are reflected in the glass doors of the display cabinet.

The music is wonderful, thinks Darius to himself. *Unbelievably beautiful!* He closes his eyes. But then he opens them again, because he has to keep looking at Mey-Mey, at the soft yellow sash that she wears tied around her neck, and which falls in two long bands over her back, at her closed eyes, curved at the corners.

It takes a long time for Darius to realize that the music has ended. It seems to him as if there are still fragments of the notes hovering around the room like creatures that have been set free and are now scattering through the air. Time does not stand still, but it seems to Darius somehow to be more solid, as if it had turned to gold.

"Fantastic!" whispers Mr. Archinola. Then he swiftly leaps to his feet. "Absolutely fantastic!" he cries, clapping wildly.

Then the whole audience suddenly rouses itself as if from some deep dream.

"Bravo!" shouts a woman, also standing.

"Fabulous!" cries an old man whose glasses fall from his nose as he, too, jumps to his feet.

The first violin and Mr. Kaplan have stood up, and each of them smilingly wipes his brow and neck with a white linen handkerchief. The cellist stands up, too, and they all bow. Everyone is applauding. They clap and clap and can't stop clapping. It sounds like summer rain. Someone lets out an enthusiastic whistle.

Darius has eyes only for Mey-Mey. She, too, now bows to the cheering audience, and her face is radiant. Finally, her gaze turns to her parents. The two of them stand, very slowly. Then they raise their arms in the air and clap— louder than everyone else.

"She's my daughter," says her father.

"No, she's mine," says her mother.

"Lovely fiddling by Mey-Mey, that's what I say!" cries Queenie and gives Alice a very wet kiss.

"You're absolutely right," says Alice, laughing, and strokes her hair.

CHAPTER TWENTY-TWO
Room to Dance

Three weeks have passed since the musical soirée. After the thunderous applause, Darius plucked up courage, returned Pizzicato to Mr. Archinola, and told him the whole strange story. The blue light in the cabinet. The healing of his finger. The poor woman on the bench. His plan to help Mey-Mey, although she didn't really need his help at all. He left nothing out.

The violin-maker had been skeptical, but after what Alice had told him about the empty glass cube at the violin museum in Cremona, and after he'd inspected the yellowed sign through the f-holes in the violin itself, he seemed to be a bit more convinced. Under no circumstances, though, was he willing to test its extraordinary powers.

"Either one *makes* violins or one *plays* them," he stated with authority, "and the rest is simply nonsense." And he swore that, as sure as he was Archibald Archinola, master violin-maker, he was never going to part with Pizzicato, because only then could he make sure it never fell into the wrong hands again. Unless all of them together took the instrument back where it belonged—to the museum in Cremona.

But then he suddenly turned his attention to Darius, and he had a very serious expression on his face. "One more thing," he said. "Even though it's laudable that you wanted to do good with the violin, the fact is, you stole it from me."

"But I only—"

"Enough!" Mr. Archinola raised his finger. "There is now a violin missing from my cabinet—true or false?" he asked, pointing toward the salesroom.

"True," said Darius, feeling very guilty.

"And so it has to be replaced, does it not?"

Darius nodded.

"You are going to make a new one," said Mr. Archinola firmly. "The first violin that you make—as your qualification to be a journeyman—will belong to me, and then we shall be even."

Although Mr. Archinola had actually been telling him off, after this conversation, Darius had been happier than he'd ever been in all his life.

He was going to be a violin-maker.

Nevertheless, after all that, he had finally had to say good-bye to Mr. Archinola, Alice, and also Mey-Mey, though he had tried hard not to show how sad he was to do so.

♪ ♪ ♪ ♪ ♪ ♪

Now everything is the same as before. For his essay, "The Work People Do: Three Weeks Job Shadowing with Violin-Maker Archinola," Mrs. Helmet gave him an A, but somehow he didn't really care.

He's often haunted by thoughts of the Needhams. But by now he's almost convinced that they might not even have existed and that he had simply imagined everything that had happened.

When lessons are over, he has lunch with the others at the big table. His favorite is still hot dogs and potato salad with apple, but even while he's chewing away, he's generally thinking of something else.

Darius no longer listens to music.

On his old pink radio Queenie plays the latest pop songs and sings with her squeaky voice into a plastic microphone. In her pink room she also practices complicated dance routines and sometimes invites Darius to come and watch her, because her latest burning ambition is to be a pop star. After her encounter with Pizzicato, she has grown a whole centimeter. Everyone is amazed! And she has made up her mind to carry on growing, because then people will get a better of view of her when she's dancing.

♪ ♪ ♪ ♪ ♪ ♪

It's Friday. Outside it's drizzling. Through the open window comes the sweet smell of acacia blossoms. Darius takes his giant calendar from the desk drawer and spreads it out on the floor. He drew it himself on graph paper, and it was a lot of work: each box represents a day until he can finally leave school, which he figures amounts to twelve hundred days. That's how long he must wait before he can go and do his violin-making apprenticeship under Mr. Archinola.

He takes the top off his green felt pen and carefully draws crosses in the days that have now passed. There have been three since his last entry. Then he sticks the top back on again and gazes at the calendar. Time passes so slowly!

I can't go out cycling in this rain, he thinks, and so he takes off his shoes and crawls under the comforter. He hasn't done that for ages! It feels almost like it did before, except that he's not listening to the pink radio. But at least no one pesters him here about why he looks so gloomy and how it's time he started laughing again.

Outside there's the rumble of thunder. He snuggles down deep under the feathers and even covers his head with the comforter. A minute later, he's fallen fast asleep.

Darius dreams. Mey-Mey is playing a pink violin. She waves to him and blows him a kiss. Queenie performs a dance with a fire extinguisher and afterward bows to the audience with it. Mrs. Needham beckons to him with a bony finger. Her poisonous snicker makes his heart pound. But at the moment when his fear is so great that he wants to wake up, Mr. Archinola appears to him in his dream. Loudly he clears his throat and says, "Violin-Maker Archinola speaking. Can you hear me, Darius?"

Darius wants to shout "Yes!" and tries to do so, but not a sound comes out of his mouth.

"Can you hear me, boy? If you don't answer, I'll have to leave!"

Darius tries one last time with all his strength to call out, but he simply can't do it. Then, with a start, he wakes up. With his heart knocking, he stays under the comforter. Outside, the rumble of thunder is now louder, and the rain is beating down.

"Boy?" says a voice.

Darius lies there as stiff as a plank of wood.

"It's me. Is that you under there?"

Slowly Darius pushes back the comforter.

In front of him, big and bearded, stands none other than Mr. Archinola!

Darius leaps from his bed and reaches out his hand to Mr. Archinola, who grasps it. But instead of shaking it, he holds it for a long time in his own.

"Let's sit down for a moment," he says at last. He perches on Darius's rumpled bed and pats the spot beside him. "Now tell me how things have been for the last three weeks."

Feeling both shy and happy, Darius sits down next to him. This time he feels as if it's not just his shoulders but his whole body that's made of porcelain.

"Okay," he says softly. He just can't think of anything cleverer to say, which is irritating.

"Okay, uh-huh, well, that's good," mumbles the violin-maker. He straightens his pant legs even though they're not crooked. And he strokes his beard even though he gave it a thorough brush this morning.

Suddenly he pulls a folded piece of newspaper out of his coat pocket, spreads it out, and passes it to Darius. "Read this."

Wonder Couple Caught

Last night, the police pulled off a spectacular arrest. The self-proclaimed Wonder Doctor Needham and his mother, who had hit the headlines for several days thanks to their sensational cures, were captured at the airport shortly before their attempted escape to Mexico City. The pair is accused of numerous cases of fraud and the kidnap of two children, whom they held captive in the cellar of their house. Among other serious offenses is the fact that the accused man had forged all his medical degrees and had no qualifications at all apart from a first-aid course for his previous job—as a haunted house operator at an amusement park. His mother had been a ticket collector. The couple denies all charges, but have been arrested on the strength of overwhelming evidence against them. Large numbers of patients of the so-called wonder doctor have filed complaints. After treatment at Needham's practice, they all fell victim to inexplicable new illnesses, for which the accused refused to take responsibility. We have been informed by reliable sources, however, that after a few days, these at times dangerous symptoms disappeared.

There is a large photo above the article, showing two policemen pushing the Needhams through the open door of a police car. Mrs. Needham's mouth is wide open, and Darius can just imagine her crying out, *"Oh, Bunny!"* Her son's reflecting sunglasses have slipped down so far that one of his horrified little piggy eyes is clearly visible.

Darius can't help grinning. "So it wasn't a dream after all."

"No, it wasn't," says Mr. Archinola and lets the article flutter to the floor, where it lies like a worthless fake certificate. The two of them say nothing for a while.

Haunted house, thinks Darius. *That fits both of them perfectly.*

"Now there's something else," says Mr. Archinola. "I'm not too good with children. But just in case you could sort of picture it, I'd…" He gets up and paces to and fro. "I'd be very happy if…" He paces even more quickly and strokes his beard as if he were a contestant in the Beard-Stroking Olympics and had reached the final strand. "If you would come and live with me," he says at last. "I mean, you could have the guest room all to yourself. There's plenty of space. It's as good as empty, don't you think?" He looks uncertainly at Darius, as if the guest room is a pretty poor offer.

Darius is speechless.

"And could you perhaps picture changing your name to…um…Archinola?"

Darius sits there as if turned to stone. Has he heard right? Can it really be true that the violin-maker wants to adopt him—the slugboy from the children's home who stupidly stabbed himself with the chisel, lied to him, and almost lost his Pizzicato?

No! he convinces himself. He must certainly have got this all wrong. Absolutely impossible. Lost in his thoughts, he shakes his head.

"Oh, all right then…" says Mr. Archinola when he sees Darius shaking his head. "I understand. I just thought you might perhaps…We could…Well, why would you want to come and live with an old block of wood like me?" He laughs with embarrassment. "It was probably, yes, a selfish thing for me to think." He cracks his knuckles, tries to smile—which makes him look really sad—stands up, and walks slowly and stoopingly toward the door.

"I wish you all the very best, my boy," he says. "Maybe you'll come and visit me occasionally."

Only gradually does the truth dawn on Darius. All the violin-maker's words land gently and make their way first to his head and then directly into his heart. After that, the little wheels in his head start turning again, and slowly he begins to think, *Darius Archinola. Darius Archinola. Darius Archi...*

"Yes," he says at last, as if he's just woken up from a strange sleep in which he's been trapped all his life. But Mr. Archinola's hand is already on the door handle, and he hasn't heard.

"Yes!" cries Darius at the top of his voice. Then he jumps off the bed and runs after Mr. Archinola. The violin-maker turns with a look of astonishment. Darius laughs. He laughs just as half an eternity ago he had laughed in the hall of House Four and had swung Queenie round and round with joy. He cries, "I would like to be called Darius Archinola! And I would like to be a violin-maker! And most of all I would like to come and live with you!"

The violin-maker stands there thunderstruck. "My boy!" he says, and the laugh lines spread all around his blue eyes. "I'm so happy! Wonderful!"

"When...When? I mean, when can I come?" asks Darius, lowering his voice.

Mr. Archinola's face is becoming brighter and brighter, like a flower that's been watered after a long period of drought.

"Have you got school tomorrow?" he asks.

"N-No."

"Then come and spend the weekend with me now, and we'll get the formalities started. For the adoption, I mean. Ben has already said he would help if you said yes," explains Mr. Archinola. He takes the boy in his arms. "Ah, my boy, I really missed you. And it wasn't just me. Alice and Mey-Mey keep asking about you."

"Boo hoooooooooooo!" A high-pitched howl suddenly enters the room. It's Queenie. She stands in the doorway, shedding bitter tears. "Boo hoooo!"

Darius frees himself from Mr. Archinola's embrace, hurries across to her, and kneels at her feet. "Queenie, what's the matter *now*?"

"Boo hoooo! You've got to wa-a-atch me when I da-a-ance! Don't go-o-o, Darry!"

Darius picks Queenie up and perches her on his hip. "I'll come and see you, I promise," he says comfortingly. "After all, we'll still be living in the same town."

"No-o-o-one ever comes to vi-i-sit me!" she wails. "You're only sa-a-aying that!"

Mr. Archinola joins them. "Queenie, I've talked it all over with Alice," he says, "and if you like, you can come and visit us every weekend and over the holidays. We'd be delighted if you agreed."

Queenie's whole body is trembling.

"What do you say?" asks the violin-maker.

"Can I...Can I also do my dancing there?" she asks tentatively, in a voice made even tinier by her crying. Then she sniffs and snuffles.

"But of course," says Mr. Archinola. "There's plenty of room for you to dance. And we'll applaud the performance, won't we, Darius?"

"Like mad!" says Darius. "Queenie's already a pretty good dancer, actually," he adds. "She practices all the time." He holds Queenie very tight, and then he lets her slide away from his arm. She takes his hand.

And now, as if he still can't believe it, Darius asks, "Can I really come and live with you?"

"Right away," says Mr. Archinola, laughing. "Pack your bag, my boy, and I'll wait here for you."

CODA

𝄞

During the holidays, Mr. Archinola, Alice, Darius, Mey-Mey, and Queenie all went together to Cremona. After they had handed Pizzicato over to Signor Mosconi, the magic violin hung once again in the Cremona museum.

One sunny afternoon, the little gray-haired curator stood in the far corner of the *saletta dei violini* in front of a large crowd of guests. He opened the glass cube, and with his fountain pen, and in his beautifully neat handwriting, he wrote on the sign below the violin:

REAPPEARED 2009.

Everyone clapped. A string quartet then played something, and Queenie—who was wearing a pink tutu—would have liked very much to perform a dance, but Alice explained that it wouldn't be quite the thing for a violin museum. Mey-Mey and Darius stood very close together, and eventually Darius plucked up the courage to take hold of her hand. She didn't pull it away, but instead held his very tightly. That made him so happy and excited that he scarcely noticed anything else of what was going on. In the meantime, Signor Mosconi delivered a very fine speech. The journalists and tourists took at least five hundred photos of Pizzicato, but the violin didn't come out very well on any of them. It looked more like a shadow. A bluish shadow. And sometimes a bluish light. It depended on who took the photograph.

♪ ♪ ♪ ♪ ♪ ♪ ♪

A few years later, Darius made his first violin. It was the one he still owed Mr. Archinola. He made it very quickly—actually, in just seven weeks. The violin-maker was astonished, because despite the speed, the violin was "almost perfect."

Darius had done it so quickly because his second violin was much more important for him. He made it for Mey-Mey. This instrument was outstandingly beautiful. Its varnish had a bluish sheen. Instead of a scroll, Darius carved the face of a girl. She looked a little like Mey-Mey.

And Mey-Mey herself? She conquered one concert hall after another, all over the world.

But Darius always knew she would.

And he was immensely proud of her for the rest of his life.

About the Author

Photo © Peter von Sághy

Rusalka Reh was born in Melbourne, Australia, in 1970 and grew up in Germany. She studied special education, rehabilitation, and art therapy in Cologne. She began her career as a scientific assistant at the university's music seminar and later worked as an art therapist in municipal children's homes. Since 2000, she has been working as a freelance author, writing lyrics and prose. In addition to books for children and adults, she has published several texts in anthologies and magazines.

About the Translator

David Henry Wilson (1937–) was born in London, and educated at Dulwich College and Pembroke College, Cambridge. He taught in France and Ghana before becoming a university lecturer in Germany, first in Cologne, then in Constance—where he founded the university theatre—and later in Bristol (England). His theatre plays have been widely produced in Britain and other countries, and his children's books (especially the Jeremy James series) have been translated into many languages. His translation work from French and German ranges from children's fiction through art and culture to literary theory and other academic fields. He is married and lives in Taunton, England, where to his wife's dismay he still plays cricket. They have three grown-up children but only one grandchild. They would like more grandchildren.